July 2021
Hi, Katie!
Hope yo~ ~e
fun th~ ~n!

BOOK 1
MY COUNTRY COUSINS
JOURNEY TO
JUNiPER
JUNCTiON

Heather & Quinn

Heather N. Quinn

☺ ☺

Cover illustration by Kit Laurence Nacua
Book design by Praise Saflor
Family Crest by Oak MacDrought

First published in 2021
Babblegarden Publishing Ltd.,
P.O. Box 58,
Navan Stn Main
Navan ON K4B1J3
Canada

Typeset in Georgia
This font specifically chosen to support reading

Publisher's Cataloging-in-Publication data

Names: Quinn, Heather N., author.

Title: Journey to Juniper Junction / Heather N. Quinn.

Series: My Country Cousins

Description: Ottawa, ON: Babblegarden Publishing Ltd., 2021. | Summary: In the early 1990's, a ten-year-old British girl travels alone to visit family in rural Canada and learns that she is stronger and more capable than she imagined.

Identifiers: ISBN: 978-1-7777124-9-5 (hardcover) | 978-1-7777124-8-8 (paperback) | 978-1-7777124-7-1 (ebook)

Subjects: LCSH Family--Juvenile fiction. | Farm life--Juvenile fiction. | Ontario--Juvenile fiction. | Canada--Juvenile fiction. | CYAC Family--Fiction. | Farm life--Fiction. | Ontario--Fiction. | Canada--Fiction. | BISAC JUVENILE FICTION / Girls & Women | JUVENILE FICTION / Lifestyles / Country Life | JUVENILE FICTION / Imagination & Play Classification: LCC PZ7.1.Q555 Jou 2021 | DDC [Fic]--dc23

This book belongs to:

....

We dedicate this book to
our wonderful families.

Dear Reader,

We've written a short story prequel to *Journey to Juniper Junction* just for you.

If you would like to read it, please take a moment to visit our website: www.heathernquinn.com and sign up with your favourite email address.

You'll receive a copy of the short story *Goodbye, Bronwyn* and you'll be the first to hear when we release a new book in the **My Country Cousins** series.

(Under 13? Please, ask your parents or guardians before you enter your email address. Thanks, kids!)

Best wishes,
Heather & Quinn

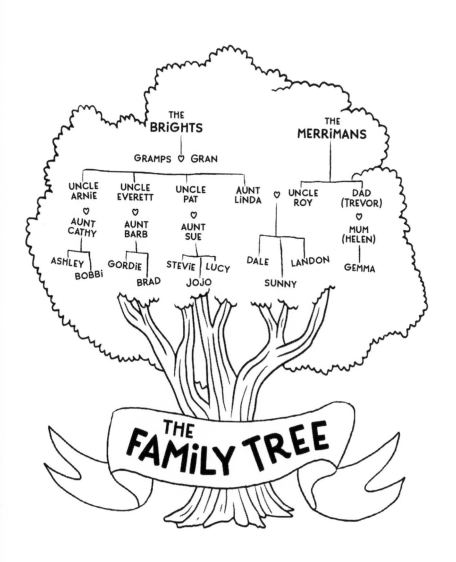

THE
BRiGHTS

THE
MERRiMANS

GRAMPS ♡ GRAN

UNCLE
ARNiE

UNCLE
EVERETT

UNCLE
PAT

AUNT
LiNDA

UNCLE
ROY

DAD
(TREVOR)

♡

♡

♡

♡

AUNT
CATHY

AUNT
BARB

AUNT
SUE

MUM
(HELEN)

ASHLEY

GORDiE

STEViE LUCY

DALE   LANDON

GEMMA

BOBBi

BRAD

JOJO

SUNNY

THE
FAMiLY TREE

1

"School will be over soon," Gemma Merriman said, as her mother placed her dinner on the table. "Do I have to go to camp this summer?"

"You've always loved camp," her mother said, sitting down.

"I used to, but it's always the same old things, and now that Bronwyn is gone I don't have anyone to go with."

Recently, Gemma's best friend, Bronwyn, had moved from Chester, England, where they had grown up together, to Sydney, Australia.

"There is another option," said her father, his eyes twinkling. Gemma leaned forward.

"What is it, Dad?"

"Your mum and I had a long talk last night and we think you're old enough for a trip."

Gemma stared in wide-eyed disbelief. All her begging had worked!

"Yes!" she cried, rocketing out of her chair. She threw her arms around her father's neck.

"I can't believe it!" she said. "We're going to Australia! I get to see Bronwyn! Oh, Daddy! Thank you!"

Her father put his arm around her, but he didn't hug her. Gemma leaned back to look at him. He and her mother were exchanging worried glances.

"What's the matter?" she asked.

"Gemma, we're not going to Australia," her father said. Gemma dropped her arms and stepped away.

"What? Why not? I thought—"

"Last night, we spoke to Uncle Roy and Aunt Linda. They've invited you to spend the summer with them," her father said. Gemma was stunned.

"In Canada?"

"It's just an idea, Gemma," her mother said. "You don't have to go. We can still find you some day camps and—"

"No, wait! I thought we were going to see Bronwyn, but if we're going to Canada—"

"Steady on, Gemma," her father said, holding up his hand. "Your mum and I will be working this summer. We aren't going to Canada. We thought you might like to go and get to know your country cousins."

Gemma knitted her brows together. "Alone?"

She sank back into her chair. At ten years old, she was aching for adventure. In fact, a day didn't go by when she didn't tell her parents about it. But this? She had never thought of something like this.

"I've only met my cousins once. It was such a long time ago. I was only five."

"Trevor, it's clear to me that Gemma doesn't want to go," her mother said. "I think we should just drop the whole idea and focus on finding her some good day camps."

"Wait!" Gemma said, sitting up. "I didn't say that. Can't we talk about it?"

She knew so little of her country cousins. Her father's younger brother, Roy, had moved to Canada before she was born. He lived in a place called Juniper Junction with his wife, Linda. They had three children: a boy named Dale, a girl named Sunny, and another boy named Landon.

She looked at her parents. Her mother looked doubtful. Her father winked and picked up his knife and fork. She followed his lead.

After taking a couple of bites of her supper, she said, "This is good shepherd's pie, Mum." She saw a smile flicker across her father's face.

He asked, "What do you remember about our visit to Canada, Gemma?"

She shrugged and shook her head.

"Oh, you must remember something," he said. "We had such a good time. Don't you recall little Landon climbing a tree and—"

"I remember! A baby was stuck in a tree and a fire truck came. A fireman had to rescue him."

"Then the fireman had to go back up the ladder and get his teddy bear," said her father. They all laughed.

That story seemed to unlock something in Gemma's brain; suddenly, she had another memory.

"This sounds crazy, but did I see a cake explode?"

"Yes!" said her mother. "Dale put a baseball right through the kitchen window, and it landed in a cake that I had just finished icing."

"That was an accident," Gemma's father said.

"It was a messy accident," said her mother.

"I was chased by a huge flock of chickens too!" Gemma declared. She shuddered at the memory of an angry flock of feathered beasts hunting her down.

"There were six chickens," her father said. "Uncle Roy gave you a bucket of scraps to feed them. They flocked around you, and you scarpered." He laughed.

"Oh," said Gemma. She chuckled bashfully.

"As I recall, Gemma found the animals and the children a bit too wild," said her mother to her father. She looked at Gemma and patted her hand. "I quite understand you not wanting to go. I said to your dad last night—"

Her father interrupted. "Roy's kids aren't wild. They're just kids. They've got a lot of freedom because they live in the country, and they have a lot of fun because they've got each other."

Gemma liked the sound of that. She didn't have a brother or sister or any nearby cousins, and sometimes she felt very much alone. She was always supervised. I'll be supervised at day camp, she thought. Worse, I'll have to try to fit in and find a new friend.

Spurred on by that thought, she burst out, "I don't want to go to camp! I liked my cousins. I want to go to Canada."

"Gemma," her mother said, setting down her cutlery and taking a serious tone. "You do understand that Canada is a long way from England, and you would have to fly there by yourself."

"I know," Gemma said. She was already trying to imagine how her cousins might have changed, and the impression she might make upon them as they greeted one another at the airport. They were sure to be impressed that she was allowed to make the trip alone. She would wear her new white skirt and her purple blouse with the silver belt and—

Interrupting Gemma's thoughts, her mother said, "It would mean spending the whole summer in Canada. You can't come home if you get homesick. Whatever happens, Gemma, you will have to stay. You do understand that?"

Her father said in a serious tone, "Your mum's right, Gemma. Looking after yourself is a big responsibility. You'll have to be sensible, and you'll have to be brave."

Gemma's tummy tightened. More than once she had called her parents to come and get her from a sleepover because she was homesick. But that was ages ago, she thought. I'm ten years old now. I'm almost ten and a half.

"I'm not a baby!" she protested. "I wouldn't get homesick. Not if I was with my cousins."

"You might," said her mother, giving her a knowing little nod. Gemma decided to change the subject.

"How old are my cousins now?" she asked.

"Dale is twelve, Sunny is ten, and Landon just turned eight," said her mother.

"Do they want me to come?" Gemma asked.

"Of course, they do!" said her father. "Your uncle Roy says they've got all sorts of fun things planned for you. He said he would get you a bicycle."

Her mother sighed and pursed her lips. Gemma gave her father a pleading look.

"Gemma, your mum and I talked last night, and we agreed that you're ready for this. Now, it's up to you. What do you think?"

"I want to go!" Gemma exclaimed.

"Oh, Gemma, are you absolutely sure?" asked her mother.

Gemma knew that she could ease her mother's mind and get her own way if she could make her smile. She had done it before. So, pretending to think hard, she put her finger on her chin and looked at the ceiling.

"Hmm," she said. "Do I want to go to boring old day camp again, or do I want to go to Canada and get to know my country cousins?"

"Well, Gemma?" asked her mother.

"Oh, Mum!" Gemma clasped her hands together. "I'm absolutely sure I want to go. It will be such an adventure. Please?"

Her mother looked at her for a moment, and then she reached out and gave her hand an affectionate little squeeze. "Okay," she said with a tiny smile.

"Then, it's settled," said her father. "Tomorrow, we'll call Uncle Roy and Aunt Linda and get everything organized."

"Oh, thank you," said Gemma, jumping up to hug her parents. She twirled around, and her long brown braid sailed out. Dropping back into her chair, she clapped gleefully.

"I can't believe it!" she said. "I'm going to Canada. By myself!"

CONGRATULATIONS!
YOU'VE READ 1,415 WORDS!

2

It was drizzling when Gemma and her parents arrived at the airport. She watched the wipers swish back and forth and followed her father's eyes in the rearview mirror as he parked the car. Her mother had been fussing all morning but since getting into the car she had been quiet. Now, she turned and gave Gemma an overly-enthusiastic smile.

"Remember, there's nothing to worry about, Gemma," she said. "We've arranged for someone to watch over you until you arrive in Toronto. Uncle Roy and Aunt Linda and the children will meet you at the airport. Are you sure you have everything you need?"

Gemma smiled at her mother; they had been over this numerous times.

"I think so," she said, holding tightly to her new backpack. She had an activity book about Canadian wildlife, and her pencil case was bulging with new markers, pencils, and pens. Best of all, she had the new art journal which her friend Bronwyn had given her as a going away gift.

Gemma let her mother hold her hand as they went into the airport. At the check-in, she watched the hustle and bustle around her. People hurried every which way pushing carts and pulling suitcases on wheels. Noisy children dashed about. Announcements echoed throughout the large space. It was all so confusing. Gemma bit her lower lip, as she always did when she was excited or nervous.

Once she was checked in, she and her parents made their way to a spacious waiting area where huge windows gave them a view of the airplanes. Her father pointed out the one she was to ride on. Gemma nodded while tightly squeezing her mother's hand.

Eventually, there was nothing to do but wait. They sat side-by-side in red plastic chairs. Gemma took out her journal and her pencil case. She sketched the waiting area, and the various people in it. Beneath her drawing, she wrote about what she had seen since arriving at the airport. It helped her to relax.

At home, she had a vast collection of journals. They were filled with all sorts of memories and feelings. Whenever she finished a journal, she put it in a cardboard box which she kept under her bed. Occasionally, she liked to look through her old journals. It was fun to read about things she had done, and to see how she and her drawings had changed.

"Look, Gemma," said her father, interrupting her thoughts. "Here comes your chaperone." Gemma looked up and saw a woman in a navy blue blazer and skirt walking briskly toward them. Shoving her journal and pencil case back into her backpack, she slid off her chair and stood waiting. The woman spoke briefly to Gemma's parents and then turned to Gemma, smiling.

"Hello, Gemma. I'm Marilyn."

"Marilyn is a flight attendant," said Gemma's father. "She's going to look after you during your trip."

They all walked together to a kiosk, where Gemma's ticket was processed. Her father gave her a long hug and kissed her cheek. Then he stepped back, resting his hands on her shoulders.

"Have fun!" he said. "We love you, and we're very proud of you."

She looked up at her mother, who was dabbing her eyes with a tissue.

"I'm sorry," her mother said, laughing ruefully. "I said I wouldn't cry."

Gemma didn't want her mother to worry about her, so she blinked away her own tears and reached out for a hug.

"I'll be fine, Mum. Really."

Her mother gathered her into a bone crushing squeeze. "Look after yourself, Gemma. We love you, so much." She let go of her and kissed her forehead.

Marilyn said, "Ready, Gemma?" Gemma swallowed hard and nodded.

She walked with Marilyn to a set of wide glass doors. They slid open, and Gemma glanced back at her parents. There they stood, arm-in-arm, smiling, and waving. She smiled and waved back.

Then turning again quickly, she followed Marilyn over the threshold, into a brightly lit corridor. Hearing the doors swish shut behind her, Gemma felt her heart quicken. There was no turning back now!

From her seat next to the window, Gemma watched the plane fill up. A young couple appeared with a smiling, gurgling, baby boy. The man sat down next to Gemma, and the woman sat in the seat by the aisle with the baby on her lap.

The man nodded at Gemma and began flipping through a magazine. The woman smiled and said, "Hello." Then she began singing softly to the baby, gently bouncing him on her knees. The baby strained to look around the plane.

Eventually, the captain's voice came over the intercom to announce they were ready for take-off. Gemma latched her seatbelt and stowed her tray. She watched out the window as the plane began rumbling toward the runway.

At the runway, they waited for a few minutes, and then the plane began moving. Gemma clutched the armrests of her chair. The plane picked up speed, roaring louder and louder. Finally, with a long, piercing shriek, it lifted off.

She watched in wonder as the tarmac shrank away. In no time, the plane was high in the sky. Far below, the people scurried about like ants between the tiny buildings. Everywhere, cars and trucks, small as toys, zipped along black ribbons of asphalt.

The city soon gave way to the countryside. It looks like a great, green patchwork quilt, thought Gemma. She imagined the hedges stitching together the farmers' fields, and the trees and bushes to be buttons and bows.

Up and up, they went. Soon, Gemma could see nothing but a veil of white fog covering her window. When it disappeared, there was the bright blue sky! She looked down. The airplane was sailing above a magnificent blanket of puffy white cloud.

It's quite magical, she thought. The clouds look like marshmallows! Pulling out her journal and some of her favourite pencils, she began drawing a silver plane soaring high above marshmallow clouds. A shiver of excitement rippled through her. I'm really doing it, she thought. I am having my very own adventure!

CONGRATULATiONS!
YOU'VE READ **2,435** WORDS!

3

"Gemma, would you like something to drink?" Gemma looked up from her journal and saw Marilyn standing with a cart. The couple sitting next to her were sipping orange juice. The baby was sucking a bottle.

"Do you have Coke?" Gemma asked.

"We do."

"Oh, yes, please!"

It was fun not having to ask permission to have a Coke. Gemma's mother was particular about fizzy drinks and junk food. Whenever Gemma asked for such things at the grocery store, her mother would say, "They're only for special occasions." Well, Gemma thought, stowing her things beneath the seat in front of her, flying over the Atlantic Ocean is certainly a special occasion.

As Marilyn poured her drink, Gemma tossed her long, brown braid over her shoulder, smoothed her white skirt over her lap and readjusted her tray.

"Thank you," she said, taking her drink.

The woman with the baby smiled at her. Gemma smiled back. I bet that lady is wondering how the flight attendant knows my name, thought Gemma, pulling her shoulders back and sitting up straighter. She probably thinks I fly by myself all the time.

She sipped her drink, and then she set it carefully on her tray.

"I'm going to the restroom," said the woman with the baby. "You stay with Daddy, Henry." She handed the baby to the man.

"Mmhmm," the man murmured, taking the baby without looking up from his magazine.

Gemma and the baby watched each other for a minute. When the baby finished his bottle, he dropped it on the floor. Gemma saw it roll beneath the man's seat. The baby craned its neck; he seemed to want to see where the bottle had gone.

"Ba!" said the baby. The man rocked the baby and continued to read.

"Ba! Ba!" said the baby, waving his chubby little arms. The man rocked him faster.

"Ba! Ba! Ba!" demanded the baby, his frown spreading over his whole face, and his body becoming rigid. The man shifted his magazine and continued rocking the baby.

Gemma wondered if she ought to interrupt him and tell him the baby had lost his bottle, but she felt too shy. She watched anxiously as the baby's eyes began to bulge and his face began to burn bright red. Just as he was beginning to resemble an overcooked tomato, he exploded, "Waa!"

Gemma drew back. The man lowered his magazine, looking about frantically.

"Waa! Waa! Waa!" the baby wailed.

Desperately, the man tried shushing the baby. He tried bouncing him on his knee. He made funny faces. The angry baby ignored him, rocking, and bucking like a furious pony, swinging his fists, and kicking his feet.

Gemma flinched as one of the baby's feet shot out and kicked an empty orange juice cup into the aisle.

"Aargh!" groaned the man. The baby's foot shot out again. This time, it connected with Gemma's Coke. She saw her cup, as if it were moving in slow motion, flip up into the air, tumble, and land smack onto her tray. Whoosh!

"Eww!" Gemma shrieked as Coke gushed into her lap.

The baby's mother reappeared, her eyes popping out of their sockets.

"Oh dear!" she said. Her hand flew to her mouth when she saw Gemma's drink in her lap.

The man thrust the baby into its mother's arms and gripped his chair. He took a shuddering breath. Back in his mother's arms, the baby stopped crying.

He gulped and sniffed a couple of times and stuck his thumb in his mouth.

Marilyn appeared. "Oh, my!" she said. "Are you alright, Gemma?"

Gemma blinked rapidly, biting her lower lip.

"Don't worry!" said Marilyn. "We'll have you cleaned up in a tick." She dashed off. Gemma put the empty cup back on her tray.

"Sorry," said the man. He winced. "Really."

"So sorry," said the woman. As they apologized, the baby sucked his thumb. His whole chubby face was beaming now, and he looked at Gemma as though they were sharing a great joke.

Marilyn returned with a stack of paper towels. As Gemma took them, she eyed Marilyn's navy blue suit with envy. She looked down at her own white skirt, now covered in cola. Note to self, she thought as she began to mop up the mess, never wear white on a plane!

CONGRATULATIONS!
YOU'VE READ **3,154** WORDS!

4

"You go to the restroom, Gemma, and do your best to clean up," Marilyn said, in a sympathetic tone. "I'll take care of things here."

The couple with the baby stood in the aisle. Gemma looked at her drenched skirt. Did Marilyn really expect her to walk all the way to the back of the plane looking like this? How embarrassing! But what else could she do? It would be ridiculous to sit in a soggy seat covered in Coke for the rest of the flight.

She shimmied into the aisle, cringing as the Coke trickled down her legs and into her sandals. The man and the woman with the baby looked at her with sad eyes. Marilyn handed her more paper towels and she used them to shield herself as she walked to the restroom.

Everyone on the plane must have heard the commotion. They all gawked at Gemma as she made her way down the aisle. "What a mess!" said a man with a bald head. "The poor thing!" said a teenage girl to her friend. "Ha! Ha! Ha!" laughed a little boy with his finger up his nose. His mother shushed him. Gemma hurried on.

Inside the restroom with the door locked, Gemma looked at herself in the mirror. Her face and her blouse were freckled with pop, and her skirt looked like a piece of preschool artwork.

Her lip trembled, and the next thing she knew she was crying. She couldn't help it. She had so wanted to make a good impression on her cousins. She wanted them to see how grown-up she was. Now, what would they think?

Realizing she had no choice but to get on with it, she dried her tears and did her best to clean up. She splashed water on her face and then dabbed her blouse with a wet paper towel. Slipping off her skirt, she tried to rinse it in the sink. It was no use; the Coke stain remained.

Desperately, she wrung it out and quickly pulled it back on. It felt cold and wet, and it stuck to her legs. "Eww," she said, cringing.

Bang! Bang! Bang! Gemma jumped. Someone was banging on the restroom door.

"Just a minute!" she called in a wobbly voice. Flustered, she felt herself tearing up again. Then, in her mind, she heard her father saying, "You'll have to be sensible, and you'll have to be brave."

Dad is right! Gemma thought. Turning to look at her blotchy reflection in the mirror over the sink, she told herself, "You're on your own, Gemma. You've got to look after yourself. You can't start bawling every time something goes wrong."

Bang! Bang! Bang! She glared at the door and took another moment to splash cool water on her face before throwing it open. There was the little boy who had laughed at her. He looked her up and down, wrinkling his nose. She narrowed her eyes at him and stepped out of the restroom.

Pretending she hadn't a care in the world, Gemma lifted her head, straightened her spine, and began the long walk back to her seat. As she passed the two teenage girls, she glanced at them. They smiled at her and gave her two thumbs up. She smiled back and went on. I can do this, she thought. I'm going to be okay.

The rest of the flight turned out alright. Baby Henry slept. Gemma was given a dry cushion for her seat and Marilyn replaced her Coke. All the flight attendants treated her like a princess. Each time one of them passed by, they gave her a cookie or something chocolatey or a bag of salty snacks. By the time the plane touched down in Toronto, she figured she had enough treats to last all summer. Better still, her skirt was almost dry.

She stayed in her seat and watched the other passengers gather their bags. Marilyn had said she would escort her off the plane once everyone else was off. The man and woman with the baby got up and joined the crush in the aisle. The man began collecting luggage from the overhead bins while the woman stood with the baby on her hip.

"Wave bye-bye, Henry," the woman said to the baby. He sucked his thumb and gazed sleepily at Gemma. "Thank you for being so understanding," said the woman.

"It's okay," said Gemma. "Babies can't help being messy."

"True," said the woman with a laugh. "But you were awfully good about it." She dug in her purse and pulled out a shiny red pen with a gold clip. Baby Henry tried to grab it, but she kept it out of his reach.

"I noticed you were writing during the trip," she said. "I'd like you to have this." She held the pen out to Gemma.

"Are you sure?" Gemma asked. It was pretty, and it looked expensive.

"Absolutely," the woman said. "It's the least we can do. Baby Henry wants you to have it. Don't you, Henry?" The baby tried to grab the pen again.

Seeing him scowl, Gemma accepted the pen. She didn't want him creating another scene.

"Thank you," she said. She took a moment to admire with it. When she looked up, she saw the little family being swept along the aisle by the steady flow of passengers.

"Thank you," she called again, but they were gone.

CONGRATULATIONS!
YOU'VE READ **4,052** WORDS!

5

Walking into the airport arrivals lounge, Gemma glanced anxiously around at all the different faces. The huge space thronged with emotion as people greeted one another, hugging, and laughing, and talking loudly. Gemma chewed her lip nervously, positioning herself slightly behind Marilyn, and doing her best to hide her skirt with her backpack.

"Look, Gemma," Marilyn said. Gemma looked. There were Dale and Sunny and Landon holding up a banner with the words "Welcome to Canada Gemma" painted in red letters across it. Behind the children, Aunt Linda and Uncle Roy stood scanning the crowd.

Gemma thought they looked very much as they had in the photograph which Aunt Linda had sent. Dale was a tall, skinny boy with a thoughtful narrow face and dark brown hair. Sunny was shorter, with an alert, cheerful expression. Her auburn curls were tied in a ponytail that bobbed as she looked about. Landon was a smaller version of Dale except he wore glasses. Aunt Linda had a friendly face and shoulder-length hair the same colour as Sunny's. Uncle Roy looked a lot like Gemma's father with thick dark hair and wire-rimmed spectacles. They were all dressed very casually in shorts and T-shirts.

With each step, Gemma's heart beat harder and faster. Was she excited or scared? She wasn't sure. If only my skirt weren't such a mess, she thought.

Suddenly, her eyes met Sunny's, and she knew at once that she had been recognized. A huge smile lit up her cousin's face.

"It's Gemma!" Sunny cried. She dropped the banner and began running. Landon dropped the banner too and chased after her.

"I can't believe you're here!" Sunny said. She threw her arms around Gemma, hugging her tightly and squishing her backpack. Gemma returned the hug gratefully. Looking over Sunny's shoulder, she smiled at Landon. She could see Dale winding up the banner.

"I get to hug Gemma too," Landon said, launching himself onto the girls and practically knocking them over. Dale came up, smiling.

"Hey, Gemma," he said, saluting her with the rolled-up banner. Uncle Roy and Aunt Linda followed, joining in the hug, and pulling Dale in too.

Marilyn waited until the family finished their greeting and then she said goodbye. Aunt Linda put her arm around Gemma's shoulder.

"Was it a good flight?" she asked. "It looks as though you had a bit of an accident."

Gemma glanced down at her skirt. Briefly, she told the family what happened, doing her best to put a funny spin on the whole thing. Everyone sympathized as they laughed.

"Weren't you embarrassed?" Sunny asked, her green eyes sparkling.

"I was horribly embarrassed," Gemma admitted.

"This'll make you feel better!" Sunny spun around to reveal a big tear in the seat of her shorts. Gemma's mouth fell open in surprise. Sunny spun back around. "I was doing cartwheels outside when I heard it go *rrrip!*"

What a confident girl, Gemma thought. I don't think I know anyone who would be able to laugh off a thing like that, especially if it happened in a place like this!

"Come on, you nutbars," said Uncle Roy in a jolly voice. "We have to collect Gemma's luggage and let her parents know that she's arrived safe and soggy."

As they started for the baggage area, Sunny whispered in Gemma's ear, "Tell me if you can see my underwear when I walk." She scooted ahead and glanced back over her shoulder. Gemma shook her head and Sunny waited for her to catch up.

"I'm really glad you're here, Gem," she said, linking arms. "I think we're gonna have the best summer ever."

Gemma smiled. With a friendly, confident cousin like Sunny leading the way, she thought so too.

Leaving the air-conditioned airport building, Gemma was shocked by the intensity of the July sun. Canada was much hotter than England in the summer, and it was humid too. She squinted and shaded her eyes with her hand.

"It's so hot and bright here," she said. "I bet we could fry sausages on the pavement!"

"Hey! We should try that," Sunny said.

"Don't give her any crazy ideas, Gem," said Dale. "She's got enough of her own." He gently knocked Sunny on the back of the head with the rolled-up banner. She waved him away like an annoying fly.

Gemma smiled at them. They're playful, she thought. I like their accents, and the way they call me Gem. They act like they've known me forever.

Landon, who was running ahead, turned and called to Gemma, "There's our van." She looked to where he was pointing. She was astounded.

"You have a bus!"

"It's a minivan," said Landon. "Haven't you ever seen a minivan?"

"But there's nothing mini about it," said Gemma as she came up to it. She looked around. "Everything in Canada is so big!"

Uncle Roy laughed. "I thought the same thing when I first came here," he said, loading Gemma's luggage into the back of the van. "It's a big country. Things here are much bigger than things in England. But you'll soon get used to it."

Dale slid open the side door of the van. He and Landon climbed in. They made their way to seats at the back. Gemma followed Sunny onto a bench in the middle.

"The steering wheel is on the wrong side," Gemma said.

"It's on the right side here," said Landon.

"Actually, it's on the *left side* of the car here, and it's on the *right side* of the car in England," Dale quipped. He turned, grinning at Gemma.

"Like Dad said, you'll soon get used it," said Sunny. "And them!" She jerked her thumbs towards her brothers and laughed.

Uncle Roy and Aunt Linda climbed into the van. "Buckle up," Uncle Roy called. He waited a moment. "Ready?"

"Ready!" yelled the kids.

The van began to move off, and to Gemma's surprise, all the Merrimans cried out happily, "And off we go!"

CONGRATULATIONS!
YOU'VE READ **5,044** WORDS!

6

How long until I get used to this? Gemma wondered as they joined the traffic.

"We're on the wrong side of the road," she said to Sunny.

"Not here. In Canada we drive on the opposite side to what you drive in England." Gemma's father had told her to expect this, but it was still very strange. She watched out the window, fascinated by the most ordinary things: road signs, trees, fences, and streetlights. They were all so familiar and yet so new and different too.

It was busy. There were cars everywhere, weaving in and out of several lanes. The kids made a game of spotting different licence plates, but Gemma didn't compete. She was tired. It was fun just to look out the window and listen to the excited cries of her cousins.

Eventually, they turned off the highway onto a quiet road. It wound through lush, green farmland.

Gemma was enjoying the views, but her eyes burned with fatigue. Maybe I'll just close my eyes for a minute, she thought, and leaned back in her seat.

When she opened them again she felt confused. There was the sound of gravel crunching beneath tires. She sat up and looked around. Oh, yes! It all came back in a flash. She was in Canada with her cousins. They were in a van. It was slowing down. She looked outside and saw a playground.

"You woke up just in time," Sunny said. "We're going to have a picnic."

"Where are we?" Gemma asked.

Dale stuck his head between the two girls. "We're at a park," he said. "We always stop here on long car trips to stretch and have something to eat." Gemma was pleased. She had been sitting all day. She was keen to get out and move around.

The playground was big and empty. Gemma followed the others, scrambling over the monkey bars and then racing to the swings. She saw Aunt Linda spread a blanket on the ground beneath the shade of an enormous tree. Uncle Roy took a cooler from the back of the van and set it on the blanket.

"Let's all swing at the same time!" Sunny said. Pumping their legs in unison, the children were soon soaring side-by-side high above the playground, creating their own refreshing breeze.

They swung higher, and higher. Gemma loved it! Suddenly, Dale shouted, "Now!" and he, Sunny and

Landon leapt off their swings. They flew through the air at a spectacular height and landed on their feet so hard and fast that they had to run to stay upright. Gemma continued swinging, her legs dangling now.

"Dale!" Aunt Linda called. By the tone of her aunt's voice, Gemma guessed Dale was going to be scolded for encouraging everyone to leap from such a height.

Dale slouched toward his mother. She stood over the open cooler.

"Dale! Landon!" she said. "You boys ate all the sandwiches!"

"What?" said Dale. "I thought you said we could have a snack."

Sunny put her hands on her hips. "Did you eat all the food when Gemma and I were asleep?"

Gemma dragged her toes in the sand beneath the swings to slow herself down and jumped off.

"Mum said we could have a snack. We just ate the stuff on the top," Dale said, as Gemma joined the family beneath the tree.

Landon asked, "Aren't there more sandwiches packed under the drinks?"

Aunt Linda raised her eyebrows. "Why would I pack sandwiches under heavy bottles?" she asked. She shook her head.

"Honestly, boys," she muttered, digging into the cooler again. "Well, we'll just have to see what's left."

She pulled out two large containers of water, six cups, six apples, six small oranges and some celery and carrot sticks.

"That's it?" Sunny whined. "But I'm starving!"

Dale shrugged. "Sorry," he said meekly. "Sorry, Mom. They were really good sandwiches..." His voice trailed off.

"Yeah, sorry," Landon mumbled.

Gemma saw Aunt Linda and Uncle Roy exchange a glance. They looked annoyed. She hoped the boys weren't going to be scolded anymore, for their sakes as well as hers. Her arrival would be spoiled if anyone were to get into trouble. As Uncle Roy turned to face the boys, Gemma had an idea.

"Can I go back to the van?" she asked. Then, without waiting for an answer, she ran off.

Returning with her backpack, she unzipped the front pocket, tipped it over and began shaking. Out fell packets of crackers and potato chips, chocolate covered pretzels, cookies, and assorted candies.

"The flight attendants gave me all these snacks," she said with a laugh. "I think they felt sorry for me when I got drenched in Coke."

"Gemma saves the day," said Uncle Roy. "Hip! Hip!"

"Hooray!" yelled the happy troop.

Dale's eyes were alight with relief. "Wow!" he said. "This is great, Gem. Thanks!"

"It's like Halloween!" said Landon.

"Go ahead," said Gemma. "Take your pick. I've already had lots."

The boys reached out.

"Stop!" said Aunt Linda.

Everyone looked at her cautiously.

"I think everyone else should get first pick. Don't you?" she asked the boys. They nodded sheepishly.

"Sunny, you take first pick" said Uncle Roy. "In fact, you can take the first two picks, if that's alright with Gemma." Gemma smiled and nodded.

"Great!" said Sunny. After quickly looking everything over, she scooped up a bag of chocolate covered pretzels and a large shortbread cookie studded with chocolate chips. She beamed at Gemma.

"Don't take this the wrong way, Gem," she said, "but I'm kinda glad Baby Henry kicked over that drink!"

CONGRATULATIONS!
YOU'VE READ **5,976** WORDS!

7

The sun was low on the horizon by the time the family reached Juniper Junction. Uncle Roy slowed down to let Gemma take a look at the village. They passed a red brick church, and a long, single story building that was the children's school.

There was a hotel, some shops, a tearoom, a small supermarket, and a post office. At the end of the village was a lake and a marina filled with colourful boats. Gemma liked it.

On they went past tidy houses where tall trees stood on neatly clipped lawns. Eventually, the houses gave way to countryside. It's much wilder than the countryside in England, Gemma thought.

She said to Sunny, "Are we almost there?"

"Almost," Sunny said, as they turned onto a gravel road bordered with thick, green forest. On they went. They rounded a bend, and soon Gemma saw a grassy area with a driveway cut into the forest. A mailbox stood at the end of it. Beside it was a large wooden sign. It was painted red. White lettering spelled out, "The Merriman Family of Almosta Farm."

"Almosta Farm?" Gemma said, as the van turned into the driveway.

"There are lots of big farms around Juniper Junction," said Sunny. "Ours is just a hobby farm. We've got animals, but they're really just pets."

"So, we're *almost* a farm," said Landon. "Get it?"

Gemma nodded. "I get it." The fearsome chickens came to mind. "Uh, do you still have chickens?" she asked.

"Yep," said Sunny. "It's my job to look after them. You can help me."

Gemma wasn't ready to think about that. She smiled warily and looked out the window. Trees brushed the sides of the van as it travelled down the narrow drive. The forest here wasn't open and airy like the woodlands around her home in Chester. It was dark and mysterious, and made her think of fairy tale forests where fearsome beasts might live.

When the van left the forest, she breathed a sigh of relief. They were crossing a wildflower meadow that swept down to a lake. At the waters edge was a long wooden dock with a green rowboat tied to it.

The van passed between two huge oak trees on a front lawn and stopped before a tall, white house with lots of interesting windows and a pretty veranda with gingerbread trim. Behind the house there was a red barn surrounded by white rail fences.

"It's so pretty," Gemma said.

"There's lots to see," said Sunny eagerly.

"There is, but it's dinner time," Aunt Linda said. "Gemma, you must be exhausted after your trip. There will be time enough tomorrow for exploring the farm."

The boys and Sunny protested, but Gemma was glad that her aunt insisted they wait. Despite having napped in the van, she was tired.

The family gathered their things and Sunny threw open the van door. Gemma followed her out. She had barely set foot on the ground when she found herself face-to-face with something huge and hairy. It lunged at her!

"Ahh!" she yelled, throwing up her hands to shield her face. Remembering her Canadian wildlife activity book, her first thought was that she was being attacked by a bear. But something told her that was just silly. This animal was attacking her with nothing more than a sloppy wet tongue!

"Pepper!" shouted Uncle Roy. "Down boy! Dale, take hold of Pepper's collar."

The licking stopped and Gemma opened her eyes to see a big grey and white dog sitting before her, its amber eyes shining joyfully and its shaggy tail thumping hard against the ground.

"Sorry, Gem," said Dale. "Pepper's just glad to meet you."

"It's okay," Gemma squeaked, wiping her face. "That's the biggest dog I've ever seen. It is a dog... Isn't it?"

"He's part Irish wolfhound, we think," said Dale, stroking Pepper's head. "I found him when he was just a puppy. Nobody claimed him, so we got to keep him."

"We had no idea how big he would get," Aunt Linda said.

Pepper barked loudly, "Ro-Ro-Ro," right in Gemma's face! She cringed.

"Don't be scared of Pepper, Gem," Sunny said with a laugh. "He's just saying hello."

"He looks like a bear," Gemma said.

"He is! He's a big teddy bear. Aren't you boy?" Sunny threw her arms around the dog's neck. Pepper gave her an appreciative lick.

"He's a great watch-dog," Dale said, letting go of Pepper's collar. "We can go anywhere if Pepper's with us."

"Almost anywhere," said Aunt Linda. "But right now, we're going inside." She turned and climbed the wooden steps leading to the veranda. Pepper ran up ahead of her and danced happily at the front door.

Are they going to bring him inside? Gemma wondered as she mounted the steps. He's as big as a pony! She looked about the spacious veranda. It was decorated with comfortable-looking chairs. There were badminton birds and rackets lying about. A wind chime hanging in a corner tinkled as a welcome breeze blew through.

"Now, Gemma," said Uncle Roy, with a teasing grin, "you're one of the family, and our home is your home. But that means you must abide by the family rules."

He pointed and Gemma looked up at a wooden plaque affixed above the door. It appeared to be an ornately carved family crest. Green vines twisted around two black bears which stood on their hind legs facing each other. There were words above and below the bears.

"Would you read the words aloud, please," said Uncle Roy. Gemma licked her lips.

"If you can't behave...be funny," she said. She giggled with relief.

"It's our family motto," said Uncle Roy. "Do you think you can handle that?" Gemma smiled.

"I'll try," she said. Uncle Roy nodded.

"Good enough," he said, and opened the front door. Gemma followed Pepper inside.

8

Stepping into the house, Gemma found herself in a big country kitchen. There were balloons and paper chains tacked to the ceiling and another hand-painted welcome banner was taped to the cupboards.

Around her was chaos. Everyone talked at once. Pepper bounded about cheerfully. A fat ginger cat appeared and began winding itself around the family's legs. In a corner, two budgies chirped and flitted about in an enormous cage that had a huge tree branch in it! Over the commotion, Gemma thought she heard something else.

"Waa!...Waa!...Waa!"

She asked, "Do you have a baby?"

"We have two!" said Landon. He grabbed Gemma by the hand and ran with her down a wide hallway, calling over his shoulder, "I get to show Gemma!"

He and Gemma entered a living room followed closely by the rest of the family. In a corner of the big room was a deep aluminum drum with a frame of wire mesh over it. Landon pulled her over to it. She looked in. Peering back at her were two of the sweetest little creatures she had ever seen.

"Baby goats?" she asked.

One was white and the other was black. They had long, floppy ears and spindly legs with knobbly knees.

"Yeah," said Dale, removing the screen.

"Aren't they cute?" Sunny said as Dale and Landon quickly scooped them up.

"This is Cotton," Dale said, stroking the white goat.

"And Coal," said Landon, nuzzling the black one.

Gemma smiled at them. What funny little things, she thought, especially being in the house!

Aunt Linda looked into the drum. "Bobbi did a very good job of looking after them."

"I told you she would," said Sunny.

Gemma wondered who Bobbi was, but she felt too shy to ask.

The goats began nibbling the boys' ears.

"They're hungry," said Aunt Linda. "I'll get their bottles. Roy, would you, please, put the pizza in the oven?"

Uncle Roy saluted and followed Aunt Linda.

"Can I feed Coal?" Landon called after them.

"See if Gemma wants a go first," Aunt Linda called back.

Gemma didn't want a go. She had seen goats at petting zoos, but she had never held one.

"Why are they in the house?" she asked.

"Their mother wouldn't feed them, so our Aunt Barb gave them to us to bottle feed," Sunny said. "They have to stay in the house until they're strong."

"They look strong to me," Gemma said.

"They do now," said Sunny, kissing Coal's head. "But they couldn't even stand when we got them. Usually, goats are jumping around on the day they're born."

"Here you go, Gem," Dale said, holding out Cotton. Gemma stepped back.

"It's okay," she said. "I'd rather just—"

"Oh, come on," Dale said, taking her hand and lifting it as he settled the little goat against her chest.

Instinctively, she clutched Cotton close. He was easier to hold than she expected. She felt quite flattered when he nibbled her ear too.

Aunt Linda returned with two baby bottles. She handed one to Gemma and showed her how to hold it.

"He eats just like Baby Henry," Gemma said, smiling as Cotton sat on her lap, sucking greedily.

"When they're finished their bottles, let them stretch their legs for a bit and then put them back in the drum. Remember to wash your hands before you come to the table," Aunt Linda told everyone as she left the room.

The goats guzzled their milk in no time, and then began trotting about, kicking up their heels. Much to the delight of the children, Coal, followed by Cotton, sprang onto a nearby couch.

They pranced about on the cushions, leaping, and twisting and wagging their tails. Everyone laughed. Gemma watched in fascination. She wondered what her mum would say if she were to bring goats into the house. She wouldn't like it! She wouldn't even let Gemma get a cat for fear that it might scratch the furniture.

Aunt Linda returned, and seeing the little goats on the couch, she laughed.

"That does it!" she said. "Tomorrow, you two are going outside to live in the barn." She scooped them up and put them back in the aluminum drum. Then she smiled at Gemma.

"I'm sure you want to get cleaned up, Gemma," she said. "How about a quick shower? Uncle Roy put your suitcase in your bedroom. I'll show you the way."

"Can I come?" Sunny asked.

"No. I'm sorry Sunny. Gemma needs some space. You guys go and wash your hands, and then help Dad set the table."

Gemma followed Aunt Linda upstairs to a big bedroom where a magnificent bunk bed took her by surprise. It was framed with old timbers and built into a deep rectangular bay window. It's like a little room inside a room, Gemma thought.

"This is Sunny's room," said Aunt Linda, "but she's happy to share it with you. Tomorrow, she'll show you where to put your clothes. For tonight, you just slip on your pjs after your shower, and we'll see you downstairs when you're ready. Okay?" Gemma nodded and Aunt Linda left.

Alone, she unzipped her suitcase and began digging through the clothes that she and her mother bought for her trip. They had made such a day of it, visiting all her favourite shops, and then stopping for tea and cakes at a little café.

It had been such fun! Now, she wondered if the sundresses and skirts and pretty new tops she had chosen might be too fancy for a farm and a house with goats in the living room. She smiled when she saw that her mother had included plenty of shorts and T-shirts in her suitcase too.

I wonder if Sunny might like to share clothes, like Bronwyn and I used to do, Gemma thought. She pulled her pajamas from her suitcase and sighed. Tomorrow she would see how Sunny felt about that. Right now, all she wanted was a warm shower, some of that delicious-smelling pizza, and to go to sleep in that fabulous bed.

When Gemma returned to the kitchen, she felt a little self-conscious about being dressed in her pajamas.

"You're on this side with me, Gem," Sunny said, pulling out a chair. Gemma slipped into place and Uncle Roy set a large slice of hot pizza on her plate.

"I like your pjs," Sunny said. "They're so pretty. Do you ever swap clothes with your friends in England?"

"All the time!"

"Great," Sunny said, all smiles. "We can share clothes, if you want." Gemma nodded happily.

Aunt Linda put a salad on the table and sat down. Uncle Roy asked for quiet, and gave thanks for the meal and for Gemma's safe arrival. Afterwards, everyone clinked their glasses together noisily and the meal began.

At the end of it, Aunt Linda set a pile of small plates and forks on the table and then presented Gemma with a three-tier chocolate cake. 'Welcome, Gemma!' was piped across it in green icing.

"I hope you have room for dessert," she said.

"Oh, yes, please" said Gemma eagerly. "I have a special spot in my tummy for chocolate. No matter how much I've eaten, I've always got room for chocolate."

"Me too!" said Landon. Reaching recklessly for a fork and plate, he knocked over his glass of water.

Not again! thought Gemma. The glass went plonk, and the water poured into her lap. Landon's eyes, already large behind his glasses, widened in surprise. Everyone looked at Gemma. They seemed to be holding their collective breath.

"Oh, well," she said with a shrug. "Good thing I brought a whole summer's worth of clothing."

CONGRATULATiONS!
YOU'VE READ **8,229** WORDS!

9

The following morning, Gemma awoke to the pitter-pattering of rain on the window. She stretched and yawned and sat up, looking outside. The wet day reminded her of England, but the view was vastly different.

At home when she looked out her bedroom window she saw rooftops and tidy gardens. Here, she saw the lawn and the meadow rolling down to the lake and, far across the lake, an island covered in another mysterious forest. I wonder if anyone lives on that island, she thought.

She lay back down, enjoying the most special bed she had ever slept in. At its head was a plush green headrest and at its foot, a cubby with a charming wooden door. The bedspread was mint green. Matching curtains hung on a rod outside each bunk. She liked that she could pull them shut if she needed a private space.

Gemma wiggled her toes and pulled the bedspread up under her chin. This is a dream bedroom, she thought. The floor was made of wide, polished wooden planks. The walls were painted a pale yellow, and the trim was white. There was a chest of drawers, a bookshelf heaving with books, a toy box with a chalkboard lid and a huge desk covered in all sorts of crafting materials.

Sunny told Gemma that she and her father made all the furniture. The only thing they didn't make, she said, was the quilted bean bag chair which sat atop a braided rug in a corner of the room. Aunt Linda had made the chair and the rug from Sunny's old clothes.

Gemma told Sunny that she, too, had a quilt that her mother made from her baby clothes. She adored it and for years she used it in her dolls' pram. These days, she hardly ever played with her dolls. The quilt had faded and become soft from so much washing, but she still loved it. Now, she used it to cover the pillow on her bed. She thought, I wish I'd brought it with me.

Thunder boomed so loudly that Gemma jumped. The rain was lashing the window now. From downstairs came the sounds of people talking and moving about. She listened for a moment, and then threw back her cover and pulled herself up to look into Sunny's bunk. As she suspected, it was empty.

Slipping back into her bed, she suddenly felt lonely. Yet somehow she was reluctant to join the family downstairs. She had been given such a warm welcome yesterday, but would they be happy to see her again today?

She imagined Aunt Linda's startled expression as she came into the kitchen: 'Oh, Gemma! I'd forgotten you were here.' And what if Sunny wasn't happy to share her bedroom all summer? It was a lot to ask of anyone, really. Once the novelty of her arrival wore off, would Uncle Roy and the boys still want her around? Would any of them?

A fierce longing for home seized her. She bit her lip and found herself blinking back tears. Her breath came in shallow little puffs. Mummy was right, I'm homesick already, she thought. She squidged down in the bed, holding her cover close to her throat and wondering what to do.

She looked about. Spying her backpack with the rest of her luggage at the edge of the bed, she thought, my journal! She crawled over and grabbed her backpack. Then she dug out her journal and the pen Baby Henry's mother had given her.

Plumping her pillow and sitting back, she pressed open her journal to a fresh page and began recounting what had happened since her cousins collected her from the airport.

She was enjoying herself, smiling as she put the finishing touches on a drawing of the goats standing on the back of the couch, when she heard a light tapping on the door.

"Come in," she said shyly.

Sunny popped her head in. "You're awake," she whispered, slipping in, and gently closing the door behind her. She tip-toed to the bed, her index finger to her lips. "I'm not supposed to be up here," she said softly. "Mom said we had to let you sleep in."

"It's okay. I was just about to get up," Gemma said, closing her journal.

"Good." Sunny plopped down on the edge of the bed. "Then, I'm not doing anything wrong."

"No, don't worry." Gemma chuckled softly. "If anyone asks, I'll say I called you in."

"Is that your diary?" Sunny cocked her head.

Gemma shrugged. "I call it a journal."

"I've got a diary, I mean a journal, too," Sunny said eagerly. "I like to write poems and secrets in it. Do you keep your secrets in there?"

"Sometimes," Gemma said, instinctively pulling the book a little closer. She was reluctant to disclose just how important it was to her. She didn't know yet if Sunny was the nosy type.

"You can keep your journal in the cubby at the bottom of your bed," said Sunny. She pointed up. "That's where I keep mine."

"Okay, thanks."

"Promise me you won't look in mine, and I promise I won't look in yours," Sunny said, with a determined squint.

Gemma was relieved. "I promise."

"Pinky promise!" said Sunny, thrusting out her left hand. Gemma smiled. That was something she and Bronwyn always did too.

"Pinky promise," she echoed, interlocking her pinky finger with Sunny's, and shaking.

"Now get up," Sunny demanded cheerfully, sliding off the bed. "I'm starving. We're going to have pancakes, but we have to wait for you to come down." She tiptoed theatrically across the room, opened the door, and gave Gemma a little wave before slipping out.

Gemma stashed her journal and pencil case in her cubby and closed the door tightly before climbing out of bed. She felt happy and optimistic again. Writing and drawing in her journal had reminded her of all the fun she had had since her adventure began, and Sunny's visit had put her mind at ease. She was ready to face the day!

10

Dressed in a T-shirt and shorts, Gemma came into the kitchen. Pepper, who was lying on the floor near the bird cage, greeted her politely with a thump of his tail.

"Good morning, Gemma," said Aunt Linda, looking up from the batter she was pouring onto a hot griddle. "Did you sleep well, honey?"

"Yes, thank you," said Gemma. She glanced about. "Where is everyone?"

"In the barn. They took Cotton and Coal out there this morning. Would you like to call them in for breakfast? Go through that door and down the hallway to the porch. There's a dinner bell in there. Give it a good ring."

Gemma followed Aunt Linda's instructions and found her way to a screened porch. It had a table and six chairs in it. On one wall there was a cast iron bell with a piece of rope dangling from a clapper. She gave the rope a couple of hard yanks and put her hands over her ears. That bell was loud!

From the red barn, her cousins appeared, followed by Uncle Roy. They walked quickly through the rain, Landon leading the way across the lawn. He stamped up the steps and opened the porch door with a bang.

"Finally!" he said with a grin, kicking off his sandals. "We're all starving!"

"Hey, Gem," Dale said, following Landon into the house.

"Morning, Gem," Sunny sang, as though it were their first meeting of the day.

"Good morning, Gemma," said Uncle Roy. "Did the storm bother you last night?"

"I didn't even know there was a storm."

"I expect you were shattered after your trip. Settling in okay?"

Gemma nodded. "Yes, thanks," she said as they started back down the hall.

"Looks like the rain will last all day. Too bad since it's your first day here."

"Sunny said she'd give me a tour of the house."

"Good idea."

"I love her bed. You two made it?"

"We did. Sunny loves building things. Do you?"

"I've never tried."

"Would you like to?"

"Yes, I would, very much."

"Well, there's always something that needs building or mending on a farm, so we'll see what we can do."

He gave Gemma's hair a friendly ruffle, the same way Gemma's father often did, and they took their places at the table.

Aunt Linda set a plate of eggs, pancakes, and fruit salad before Gemma.

"Have you ever had maple syrup?" she asked, placing a jug next to Gemma's plate.

"Is it like Golden Syrup?" That was something Gemma and Bronwyn liked to have on their French toast in the morning after a sleepover.

"Sort of," said Aunt Linda. "But we make this syrup from our maple trees."

Dale said, "Come back next spring, Gem, and you can help us in the sugar shack."

"Sugar shack?" Gemma asked, looking into the jug at the thick brown syrup.

"That's what we call the shed where the sap goes when we tap the trees," said Dale.

Gemma didn't know what he was talking about.

"Do you mean all you have to do is tap on a tree and it gives you syrup?" she asked.

Everyone laughed.

"To tap a tree means to nail a spigot, a sort of pipe, into it," said Uncle Roy. "Then we attach a tube to it and tree sap flows through the tube into a vat in the sugar shack."

"Then we boil it," said Landon. "That's how it turns into syrup."

Gemma nodded, but having never seen such a thing, it was difficult to imagine. Still, she was intrigued and flattered that Dale had already invited her to return in the spring.

"What does it taste like?"

"It's really sweet and sticky," said Sunny. "Try it!"

Gemma drizzled a pool of the maple syrup onto her pancakes. She was about to place the jug back on the table close to Landon when she thought better of it. Catching Sunny's eye, she smiled and shifted it out of his reach.

"Good move," Sunny said, as though she had read Gemma's mind. "First you were covered in pop. Then you got doused in water. The last thing you need this morning is a lap full of maple syrup!"

11

When the children finished clearing the breakfast table, Sunny said, "Come on, Gem. I'll show you the rest of the house."

They started in the room where the goats had been. The windows were open a crack and the aluminum drum was gone. The air smelled fresh and clean, like the rain outside.

Sunny sighed. "The living room is so different without the goats," she said. "Kind of boring."

Gemma agreed that the baby goats had livened up the place, but she still thought the room was lovely. She walked about admiring the antique furniture and the beautiful paintings.

A painting above the fireplace, which she hadn't noticed in all the excitement the evening before, caught her eye.

"That's your house, isn't it?"

"Yes, Mom painted it. She's an artist," Sunny said with obvious pride.

The girls went for a closer look.

"It's very well done," said Gemma thoughtfully. "The house looks just as it did when we arrived last night. Your mum has captured the light beautifully."

"You talk like an artist," Sunny said.

"I like to draw and paint, but I'm not good like your mum."

Sunny crooked a finger. "Come and see her studio."

She led Gemma to another room on the ground floor. The doorway was covered in a curtain of multicoloured beads. They clattered as the girls stepped through them into a spacious room.

Two walls of windows met in a corner and before them stood an easel. The easel, and everything else in the room, was bathed in the silvery light of the rainy day. It's a proper studio, Gemma thought, getting goosebumps.

She looked about, admiring everything from the well-worn paint smock draped over a chair, to the shelves heaving with art supplies. Beneath the shelves, stacks of canvases leaned, some painted, and others bare. Framed paintings of woodlands and farmlands decorated the final wall.

Gemma wrapped herself in a hug, rubbing her arms as she walked around the room, awestruck.

"I love this room," she said. "I've never seen anything like it."

"You should see it when the sun is out."

Gemma admired her aunt's framed paintings. "Your mum is so talented."

"Mom says talent doesn't really come into it."

"Oh, but surely it does," Gemma protested, looking at Sunny. "I could practice for a thousand years, and I doubt I'd ever be this good."

Sunny turned and walked across to where the canvases were stacked against the wall. She began flipping through them. Finally, she pulled one out and held it up. It was a poor rendition of a big red barn.

"Is that your barn?" asked Gemma.

"Uh-huh."

"Who painted it?"

"My mom."

"What?"

Gemma went for a closer look. The perspective was all wrong, and the colours were muddy.

"This is Mom's first attempt at painting," Sunny said. "Now, whenever one of us starts complaining that we're no good at something she goes and gets this painting and reminds us we have to keep trying." Sunny laughed good-naturedly. "We're like: Not the painting, Mom! We know! We know! Practice makes perfect."

Gemma smiled and tilted her head, considering the picture. "It's hard to believe your mum did this painting and the one that's in your lounge."

"Lounge?"

"The room you call your living room," Gemma said, smiling again. "We call it a lounge."

"Oh, yeah, Dad says that sometimes. Not as much as he used to – Hey! You know what we should do? We should make a list of all the different words we have for the same things." She spun on her heel and replaced the barn painting. "I love making lists!"

"Yes, okay," said Gemma. Her eyes were roving around the studio again. "Does your mum ever let you paint in here?"

"Sure. We've got loads of paints and brushes and stuff we can mess around with." Sunny gently kicked a cardboard box filled with art supplies. "We can use anything we like in here."

"Shall we do some painting now?" Gemma asked.

"No, let's save that for later. Maybe after lunch. We could list all the different words we use, and then we could draw the stuff that goes with them. We could make it into a book!"

Gemma shrugged. It wasn't what she had in mind when she asked if they could paint, but it did sound like fun.

Sunny startled Gemma, suddenly thrusting out her arm, as though she were brandishing a sword.

"Now, on with the tour!" she stated grandly.

Gemma was beginning to wonder if Sunny might be a tiny bit bossy. She certainly had a flair for the dramatic. With a wistful backward glance, she followed her out of the studio.

CONGRATULATIONS!
YOU'VE READ **10,722** WORDS!

12

Continuing the house tour, the girls went upstairs. Dale called out to them. He was in the bedroom he shared with Landon, standing by a long wooden chest between two beds. Landon lay on his back on one of the beds reading a comic.

"I was just telling Gem about Mom's Practice Makes Perfect painting," said Sunny. "Are you practicing?"

Dale nodded. He set a drinking glass filled with rice on top of the wooden chest. What could he possibly be practicing with that? Gemma wondered.

"Dale is into doing magic tricks," Sunny said, sitting down next to Landon. She patted the bed and Gemma sat too.

"You've even got the proper outfit!" Gemma exclaimed. Dale took a black cloak from the back of a chair.

"It was a Christmas present," he explained, throwing it on. He picked up a wand and piece of cloth from a nearby desk. These he set on the chest next to the glass of rice.

"Do you want to see something cool?" he asked. Gemma nodded.

"Ordinary grains of rice," he said, taking the glass and scattering some rice onto the floor. He set the glass back on the chest and picked up the cloth and the wand.

"An ordinary handkerchief," he said, turning it, so his audience could see both sides.

"Now, who wants to see me turn that rice into chocolate caramels?"

Sunny and Landon's hands shot up. "Me! Me!" they shouted. Gemma glanced at them and timidly raised her hand too.

Dale draped the handkerchief over the glass of rice and tapped it deliberately three times with the wand.

"Hey, presto!" he said, removing the handkerchief with a flourish. The rice was gone! In its place there were foil-wrapped caramels!

The children cheered and Dale, grinning happily, tossed each of them a candy.

"That was brilliant!" Gemma cried.

"Show Gemma how you make things disappear," Landon urged. "It's *really* amazing."

"Yeah," said Sunny.

"Would you like to see me make a person disappear?" he asked. Gemma didn't believe he could do that, but she nodded anyway.

Dale opened the lid of the long wooden chest.

"I have here what appears to be an ordinary, empty box," he said. He pointed at Gemma with his wand. "Would you like to come and examine it?"

Gemma slipped off the bed and glanced inside.

"Care to get in?" Dale asked. Gemma, who didn't like small spaces, shook her head, and stepped back.

"I'll do it!" Landon said, hurtling himself forward. He scrambled inside. Sunny giggled as Gemma returned to sit beside her.

Dale closed the lid of the chest and speaking loudly at the box, asked, "Landon Merriman, are you prepared to enter the other realm?"

"I am," came a muffled reply. Dale waved his wand around the chest, then rapped three times on its lid.

"Hey, presto!" he said, flinging it open. Sunny pulled Gemma up and they looked inside. Landon was gone!

Gemma's mouth dropped open. "Where is he?"

Dale gave an exaggerated shrug and closed the lid. "I am simply the conduit through which these wonders work."

Gemma gave Sunny a puzzled frown.

"He talks like that when he's getting carried away," Sunny muttered.

From somewhere, Gemma heard a distant laugh. She looked at Dale.

"That's Landon laughing," she said.

"Uh, yeah, it is..."

Landon's laughter grew louder, and Dale glared at the chest.

"I command you to return," he said, waving his wand and rapping again on the chest. When he yanked open the lid, the box remained empty, but the laughter continued.

"Oooo, I can't find my way back," Landon called in a ghostly tone.

"Landon's trying to steal the show," Sunny said.

"Where is he?" Gemma asked. Sunny shrugged, her glittering green eyes round as coins.

Dale closed the lid of the box, rapped again with exaggerated patience, and growled, "Come back, if you know what's good for you." When he opened the lid this time, there was Landon, grinning like the cat who had swallowed the canary.

"Get out," said Dale. Landon climbed out and bowed to the girls. Dale pretended to kick him in the seat of his pants. Gemma laughed; they were a funny pair.

"How did you do that? Where did Landon go?" she asked.

"Do you really want to know?" asked Dale.

"Yes."

"Then you go next," he said. Gemma leaned back. She didn't want to get into the chest.

"It's safe!" Sunny said. "Don't worry, Gem." When Gemma didn't budge, Sunny continued, "Look, I'll go."

She climbed in and Dale went through the routine again, rapping on top of the chest, and then opening the lid. Sunny was gone.

"Sunny?" Gemma called. There was no reply. A little shiver ran up her spine. She looked at Dale.

"Okay, now bring her back," she said.

"No, you get in and Sunny will meet you on the other side," said Dale.

"The other side of what?" asked Gemma, feeling a little spooked.

"The other realm," Landon said. He raised his hands the way someone pretending to be a ghost might, and moaned, "Ooooooo..."

Dale's eyes met Gemma's. "There's nothing to be afraid of, Gem."

Having seen Landon's performance, and Sunny's willingness to get into the box, Gemma decided it must be safe, and climbed in. She stretched out on her back and looked up at Dale and Landon's faces looming over her.

"Comfy enough?" Dale asked. She nodded. "You're not going to freak out or anything when I close the lid?" She thought she might, but she shook her head.

The moment Dale closed the lid, Gemma knew she had made a mistake. Her hands curled into fists. The tight space and the pitch blackness frightened her. Her heart began to pound. She squeezed her eyes shut and held her breath, pressing her lips together and scrunching up her face. Each ominous tap of the wand ratcheted up her fear. I want out, she thought. I want out! I want out!

She opened her mouth to unleash a scream when suddenly the wall of the box fell away. Gemma's eyes sprang open and pale light flooded into the box. "Sunny!" she cried, seeing her cousin crouching at what appeared to be the mouth of a small cave.

"Gemma?" said Sunny, reaching in to help her out. "You're white as a sheet!"

Gemma tumbled out of the cave onto a soft blue carpet. Carpet? she thought. What sort of a cave is carpeted?

"Are you okay?" asked Sunny. Her forehead was creased with concern, but her eyes sparkled with laughter. "You weren't really frightened. Were you?"

"I'm a bit claustrophobic," Gemma admitted.

"Oh, no," Sunny said, giving her a hug.

Gemma gazed over Sunny's shoulder. They were in a round room, its walls covered from floor to ceiling in books. One of the bookcases moved. Dale and Landon burst into the room.

"Oooooo," said Landon, still playing the goofy ghost. "Welcome, Gemma, to the other realm!"

CONGRATULATIONS!
YOU'VE READ 11,883 WORDS!

13

"Cut it out, Landon," Dale said, cuffing his brother playfully on the back of the head.

"Hey!" Landon protested.

"You okay, Gem?" Dale asked.

Gemma laughed nervously. "I'm fine now. Where are we?" She looked around again.

"In the library," said Sunny.

Gemma turned, and seeing a table, she looked under it. There was a rectangular hole cut into the wall. It was the same height and length as the chest in the boys' bedroom. A door was hinged to the wall. It lay open on the floor beneath the table.

"A secret passageway?" Gemma asked.

"Yes," said Dale. "Dad built it for us."

"But how did it open when I was in there?"

"I opened it," said Sunny. "The door is held closed with magnets. It's easy enough just to push it open from inside the box if you know how to do it. Otherwise, you need someone on this side to pull on the handle. Don't worry, if you'd gone first, I would've come in here and opened it for you."

Sunny slipped under the table and closed the door.

"And look here," said Landon, dragging Gemma by the hand to the door that he and Dale had come through.

Gemma followed him out into a hallway. The walls were panelled in dark wood. Landon closed the door and it disappeared into the panelling. She touched the wall.

"You'd never know there was a door," she said.

"Pretty cool, eh?"

"It's brilliant!"

The wall opened and there was Sunny. She beckoned them back inside the library.

"I can't believe you have a secret room," Gemma said. She looked up at a ladder that was set on rails that went all the way around the room. "Is this so you can get to the top shelves?"

"Yeah," said Dale. "Want to go for a ride?"

Gemma looked up. She still felt a little shaky from her experience in the chest, but she had never been afraid of heights. Boldly, she stepped onto the ladder and climbed up.

Looking down at the children she saw their eyes shining up at her in what she imagined was admiration. She smiled at them.

"Ready?" Dale asked. She nodded. "Hold on!" he said, and taking hold of the ladder, he ran fast pulling it behind him.

Gemma clung on, laughing as her long brown braid sailed out behind her. When Dale let go, he spun into the centre of the room, collapsing close to where Sunny and Landon sat cross-legged watching. The ladder whizzed along the rails for a moment more, and then gradually slowed to a stop.

"Phew!" Gemma said. "That was as good as a fair ride."

"My turn!" Landon said, jumping up.

"Not now," Dale said. "We're still showing Gemma around."

"I'm showing Gemma around," Sunny said, getting quickly to her feet. "Come on, Gem!"

Gemma climbed down on wobbly legs, slightly dizzy after her ride. She stumbled over to where Sunny was running her fingertips along the spines of a row of books.

"This is my favourite one," Sunny said, her fingers resting on a big red book. Gemma leaned in.

"Let the Fun Begin," she read aloud.

Sunny pulled on the book, but instead of sliding out it tipped like a lever, and the bookshelf swung away from the wall.

"Another secret door?" Gemma said. "This house is amazing."

Light spilled down a wooden staircase illuminating walls that were covered in colourful painted murals. Landon pushed in and started up, followed by Sunny, Gemma, and Dale.

The stairs were painted to look like a stream. On the walls, as they climbed, a painted meadow gave way to woodland, and throughout it all were animals.

"These paintings," Gemma said in awe. "Did your mother do them?"

"Yes," said Sunny. "I helped."

"Sunny passed Mom the paint," Dale said with a laugh.

"I did some of the flowers," Sunny protested.

Landon looked over his shoulder. "We helped Dad and Uncle Pat build the library too. The secret doors were my idea," he said. "Dad just had to figure out how to build them."

Gemma heard Dale chuckle. She glanced back over her shoulder, and they exchanged a smile.

At the top of the stairs, Gemma said, "It's like being at the top of a lighthouse." They were in a room with large windows on all four sides. She turned to take it all in.

A model train set dominated the space. Looking down on it, Gemma was reminded of the view from the airplane. Dale flipped a switch, and three different trains started up. They zipped about the tracks, going over bridges and through tunnels, passing farms and villages where tiny figurines of people and animals were gathered.

"It's enchanting," said Gemma, who loved miniature worlds.

"Wait till you see it at night when all the lights are on in the buildings," said Dale.

"I'll bet that's magical!" Gemma said.

"Come and see the view, Gem," Sunny said.

Gemma followed her to the first set of windows. "Wow!" she said. "You can see for miles."

"From up here, we can see all our families' farms."

"All your families?"

"Yeah, Mom's side of the family all live around here." Sunny pointed out the window. "That blue house over there is where Mom grew up. See the orchards? They all belong to our grandparents. You'll love our grandparents. Everybody does."

Gemma followed Sunny to the next set of windows. "The red brick house on the hill is Uncle Pat and Aunt Sue's place. They've got three kids. Lucy is a little baby, and Stevie and Jojo are two-and-a-half."

"Aww, a baby and twins," Gemma said, clasping her hands together and nestling them under her chin.

"Yeah, their house is nuts," said Sunny.

Baby Henry popped into Gemma's mind, and she dropped her hands. Maybe that would be nuts, she thought.

At the next wall of windows, Sunny pointed to a brown bungalow. "That's Uncle Everett and Aunt Barb's farm. They raise goats and alpacas; they gave us Cotton and Coal. Their sons, Gordie and Brad, hang around with Dale and Landon, so you'll see a lot of them."

Gemma nodded, wondering when she would meet them and what they would be like. She hoped they would be friendly.

Sunny pointed again. "See that green house? That's Bobbi's house. Her sister, Ashley, is sixteen; we hardly see her these days. Her mom and dad are my Aunt Cathy and Uncle Arnie. Bobbi's great! She's the same age as us. You'll like her. She's not only my cousin; she's my best friend."

Gemma felt her heart sink. Most girls don't like sharing their friends, she thought, especially their best friends. How will this girl, Bobbi, feel about me? Will she be nice? Or will she be mean?

Staring at the green house in the distance, Gemma sucked on her lower lip. Her mother's words echoed in her mind: "Whatever happens, Gemma, you will have to stay."

CONGRATULATIONS!
YOU'VE READ **13,045** WORDS!

14

The following morning after breakfast, Sunny picked up a pail of kitchen scraps and a basket from the counter. She handed Gemma the basket.

"I can't wait for you to meet the girls," she said cheerfully. Gemma lifted a corner of her mouth in a half smile and reluctantly followed Sunny outside. It was time to meet the chickens – she had been dreading this moment. I don't want to go into a dark, smelly barn full of bad-tempered birds, she thought.

As they crossed the lawn, Pepper bounded toward them. Gemma readied herself for a collision, but he shot past her. He gave Sunny an enthusiastic welcome, lifting her hand with his big head. She patted him and he loped off again without even glancing at Gemma.

She felt confused. She didn't want him knocking her over, but she was a little disappointed that he hadn't greeted her. I'm going to have to try harder to make friends with Pepper, she thought.

Seeing Dale and Landon leaning on a fence, she asked Sunny, "What's over there?"

"That's the goat pen. Come and see."

As they neared the pen, Gemma was surprised to see that it was filled with toys. There were balls, a wooden seesaw, ramps leading to platforms, and giant tires half buried in the ground to create bridges.

Sunny and Gemma leaned on the fence beside the boys.

"That's so cute," Gemma said, pointing to a goat balancing on the seesaw. The goats climbed onto the tires and up the ramps onto the platforms. "They're having such fun," she said, clasping her hands to her chest and laughing joyfully. "I never knew I liked goats so much."

Uncle Roy smiled at her. He was in the pen with the goats. He looks like a ring master, Gemma thought. All he needs is a top hat! I can't wait to put this in my journal! She saw him glance up at the cloudless blue sky.

"It's going to be a scorcher today," he said, walking over to the fence. "Are you going to take Gemma for a swim? Your dad tells me you're an excellent swimmer, Gemma."

Gemma shrugged, bashfully. "I've been going to the swimming baths since I was a baby. I've got my 1000-meter badge."

"Well done," said Uncle Roy.

"You swim in a bathtub?" asked Landon, screwing up his face.

Uncle Roy chuckled. "A bath is what people in England call a swimming pool," he said.

"Hey! There's another word for our book," Sunny said, gently elbowing Gemma.

Landon asked, "Do you ever swim in a lake?"

Gemma shook her head.

"You're gonna love it," he said.

I doubt it, Gemma thought. She liked looking at lakes, but the thought of swimming in one with fish and all sorts of other slimy things gave her the collywobbles.

"We'll go swimming later," said Sunny. "First, we're going to show Gemma the rope swing."

"Correction," said Uncle Roy. "First, you're going to do your chores." He gave Gemma a friendly wink; it was a lot like her father's wink. "Hop to it," he said.

Dale and Landon ran off to help their dad clean the goat stalls and Gemma followed Sunny.

"Why didn't we look after the chickens yesterday? Do we not have to do it everyday?" she asked, crossing her fingers on both hands.

"Mom and Dad only did it yesterday because it was your first day here," Sunny said. "But the chickens are my responsibility. I love them!"

Gemma uncrossed her fingers and frowned. Then she had an idea! She looked at Sunny, her brown eyes wide and hopeful.

"Maybe I should help with the goats," she said. "There seem to be a lot of them."

"No," Sunny said with a smile. "You'll like the chickens too. It doesn't take long to look after them. We just have to feed them, collect their eggs, and clean the coop."

Clean the coop? Yuk! thought Gemma.

They stopped at a fence around a large grassy yard. In the middle of the yard was an enormous cage, and inside the cage was a big red box on stilts. There was a ramp going from a trap door on the front of the box down to the ground.

"This isn't at all what I imagined," Gemma said, as she and Sunny went through a gate into the yard.

Sunny opened the cage door.

"It's like a fortress," Gemma said, following her inside. "Is it meant to keep out bears?"

Sunny looked both amused and confused.

"There aren't any bears around here," she said, scattering the bucket of food scraps on the ground. "Bears live in the woods."

"But look at all the woods around here. My mum said I shouldn't go into the woods here because there are bears."

"Not in little woods like these. Bears need big forests. If we're lucky, we might see a bear when we go camping."

"We're going camping?"

"We go camping every summer."

"I don't want to go camping if there are bears around," Gemma squeaked.

Sunny laughed. "Don't worry. Most people never see a bear, not even when they're camping."

Sunny yanked on a cord and the chicken coop's trap door banged open, dashing all thoughts of bears, and camping, from Gemma's mind. She braced herself for a mad rush of hungry birds coming down the ramp. Instead, a single chicken popped out its head. Then another head appeared and another. The chickens cooed and clucked pleasantly.

"That's Beverly," Sunny said, as a fat brown hen started cautiously down the ramp. "She's a Rhode Island Red."

"Beverly is a funny name for a chicken."

"She's named after Beverly Cleary. We named all the chickens after famous children's authors. Look, that's Anna Sewell. She's a Brahmas. And Lucy Maude Montgomery is a Buff Orpington. Here comes Judy Blume. She's an Australorp."

"Australorp?" Gemma started laughing. "That sounds like a dinosaur. You're making these names up!"

Sunny laughed too. "I'm not! Oh, look! There's Laura Ingalls Wilder. She's a Wyandotte." Sunny peered into the coop. "Now, where is Enid Blyton? There she is! Enid is a Faverolles."

Enid, a fat white hen with a frill of white feathers around her face and feet, delicately picked her way down the ramp. She joined the rest of the flock gobbling up the scraps that Sunny had spread about.

Gemma listened and watched as Sunny went on feeding the birds and explaining their daily routine. They weren't nearly as numerous, nor as smelly and scary, as she remembered. Somehow, their comical names made them less intimidating too. Still, she didn't entirely trust them, and moved warily among them.

"While they eat, we'll collect the eggs and clean the coop. Grab that basket, Gem." Sunny opened a door on the side of the coop and Gemma looked in at four nesting boxes, each containing at least one brown egg.

"They look so delicate," she said. Of course, she had seen chickens' eggs all her life, but only in cardboard egg crates at the shops. Here, in their nests, each one looked like the tiny miracle it was.

One egg had a fluffy brown feather stuck to it. Gemma thought how lovely it looked. She imagined what a pretty picture it would make, especially painted in water colours.

Sunny picked up an egg and put it gingerly into the basket Gemma held.

"Go on, Gem." She nodded encouragingly. "Pick them up the same way you would if you were in the kitchen."

Gemma reached in and carefully collected a lightly speckled, pale brown egg. "It's warm," she said.

"Must've just been laid," said Sunny, crouching and opening a cupboard under the coop. The chickens, having finished the kitchen scraps, dashed over, flocking around Gemma's feet. One jumped onto Sunny's back.

"Watch out!" Gemma cried.

Sunny laughed and glanced over her shoulder. "Judy's just being nosy," she said standing up. The chicken flew clumsily in Gemma's direction. Gemma cringed and ducked. When she straightened up, Sunny was standing holding a big bag.

"Mealy worms," she said. "They're like candy for chickens. Watch."

Sunny dug out a handful of the desiccated worms and offered them to the birds. They pecked furiously at her palm.

"Doesn't that hurt?" Gemma asked as Sunny dug into the bag again.

"Not a bit! Here, you try." Sunny held out the open bag. Gemma recoiled and shook her head.

"Oh, come on. If you're going to be a country kid, you can't be afraid of a few dried worms."

"It's the chickens. They make me nervous," Gemma admitted.

"Why?"

"Last time I was here they chased me."

"Did they?" Sunny laughed. "Trust me, you've got nothing to be afraid of. These girls are so gentle and sweet. Go on!"

Gemma felt a bit sick dipping her hand into the bag of worms. She was pleasantly surprised to discover they felt like dried coconut shavings. Taking a handful, she copied Sunny, cautiously offering her palm to the birds.

They lunged and she closed her eyes, preparing to have her fingers pecked off. Instead, she felt a gentle tapping on her palm. She opened her eyes and watched the birds' beaks bouncing off her palm until it was empty. Then they began finishing off the worms that had fallen to the ground.

"That didn't hurt at all," she said triumphantly.

The girls fed the chickens another couple of handfuls of worms and then Sunny stuffed the bag back into the cupboard.

"Come here, Beverly," she said, grabbing the big rust-coloured chicken. It flapped and struggled until Sunny subdued its wings. She cradled it. "Wanna hold her, Gem?"

The bird bobbed its head, fixing Gemma with a gimlety orange eye. She stared back at its hard amber beak, bony yellow legs, and talon-tipped feet.

"Tomorrow, maybe," she said, trying to sound nonchalant as she returned to collecting eggs. She was having a much better experience with the chickens than she had expected, but she wasn't going to push her luck!

CONGRATULATIONS!
YOU'VE READ **14,715** WORDS!

15

Gemma followed Dale, Sunny and Landon into the big red barn. On either side of them, straw bales were stacked like giant bricks, almost as tall and deep as two-story houses.

"What's it all for?" asked Gemma, looking up at the straw.

"It's bedding for our animals and the animals on our cousins' farms," Sunny said.

"But in the meantime, it's for us," said Dale, leading the way up some bales that he and his cousin, Gordie, had arranged into steps. Sunny and Landon scrambled up after him, followed by Gemma. Ouch, she thought. This straw looks soft, but it's prickly!

When Dale reached the top of the bales, he climbed up onto a platform built into the rafters. The others followed.

"It looks higher from up here," Gemma said standing on the edge of the platform. Her artist's mind loved seeing the world from a new perspective.

"It's farther across than you'd think too," said Sunny, pulling a pack of bubble gum from her back pocket. She handed it around and they all took a piece.

"You have to run really fast and push off hard when you jump," said Landon. "If you don't, you won't reach the other side. When you get to the other side, you have to push off really hard there too, or you won't make it back over here."

Gemma nodded and popped the gum into her mouth. She watched as Dale took a thick rope from a spike in the wall. He backed up to the far end of the platform.

"Is it safe?" she asked, looking up into the rafters at where the rope was tied. "It won't break?"

"It's safe," Dale assured her, tugging hard on the rope. "Dad checks it all the time." Then without warning, he ran and launched himself.

Swinging through the air, he reached the bales on the other side and pushed off powerfully. Back and forth he went, high and fast, until finally he landed nimbly on the straw beneath the platform where Gemma and the others waited.

"Monkey time!" Landon called as Dale tossed him the rope. Making sounds like an excited monkey, Landon launched himself into the air. The others laughed as he performed for them, hanging from the rope by one hand while scratching himself under his arm.

Eventually, Sunny called, "Landon! That's enough! It's our turn!"

Sunny, too, was strong and expert. She flew through the air, spinning and striking poses like an acrobat. When she landed beside her brothers, she was out of breath. Smiling up at Gemma, she tossed her the rope.

"Here you go, Gem," she called. "Remember, run fast and hold on tight!"

Butterflies fluttered in Gemma's tummy as she looked up to where the rope was tied to the rafters. She chewed her gum thoughtfully, positioning her hands just so and pulling hard to test the rope. It held the others, she silently told herself, so it will hold me. And with that thought, she ran and leapt off the platform into the air.

Nervous laughter bubbled up out of her as she sailed high above the barn floor, clutching the rope tightly and wrapping her legs around it too. Reaching the straw on the other side, she was having such fun that she forgot to kick off.

"Jump!" her cousins shouted as she swung toward them. But she couldn't bring herself to do it. She clung to the rope, and off she went again. It was a wonderful feeling to be soaring through the air. I'm like a bird, she thought.

From her pendulum, she watched as her cousins scrambled down and began dragging bales of straw into the middle of the barn floor. Finally, her progress slowed, and she found herself dangling above a makeshift mattress of straw.

Dale, Sunny and Landon stared up at her, chomping their gum thoughtfully.

"Let go!" Landon said.

"Don't try to slide down or you'll get rope burn," said Dale.

"There's no other way, Gem," Sunny told her. "Just relax and let go. You'll hit the straw and bounce. Really!"

Nibbling her gum anxiously, Gemma took one last look at the straw mattress below and closed her eyes. Releasing her grip, she dropped like a stone.

"Yowch!" she gasped as she landed with a thump in the prickly straw. A cheer went up, and she opened her eyes to see her cousins shining faces.

"You did it!" Sunny shouted.

Gemma smiled and rolled across the straw bales and onto the barn floor. Dale stretched out his hand.

"Next time, I'll jump off when I'm supposed to," she said, grabbing his hand and letting him pull her up.

"You're ready to go again?" he asked.

"Now that I know what to do, I'm sure I'll be fine," Gemma said.

"Let's go!" Dale said, leading the way. Sunny followed and Gemma ran after them with Landon close behind.

"Hey, Gem," Landon said as they began to mount the straw steps. "Something is stuck in your hair. It's right on the top, at the back of your head."

Gemma stopped and began searching her hair with her fingers. Finding something warm and rubbery, she gasped!

CONGRATULATiONS!
YOU'VE READ **15,578** WORDS!

16

"M y gum!" she cried, taking hold of it, and pulling. She looked at her cousins. Their eyes were bugging out. "It must have popped out of my mouth when I landed!"

"Don't pull it!" Sunny shouted. "You're making it worse." Gemma stopped pulling and gave Sunny a desperate look.

"Come with me," Sunny said. She grabbed Gemma's hand and they ran to the house. Inside, Gemma caught a glimpse of herself in a mirror hanging in the hall.

"Oh, no!" she wailed, stopping short. Hair and straw were matted together into what looked like a bird's nest on the top of her head. She frowned and her eyes shimmered with tears.

"Don't cry, Gem," Sunny said. "Pepper had gum in his hair once and Mom got it out."

"But your mum isn't here. She said she was going grocery shopping."

"Good! Because if she was here we might get in trouble."

"What? Why?"

"She doesn't mind if we chew gum if we're reading or drawing or something. But she doesn't like us chewing gum when we're running and playing. She says we could choke on it if we fell or something."

Thinking about that frightening possibility, Gemma was distracted for a moment. She blinked away her tears. Sunny grabbed her hand again and pulled her into the kitchen.

"Sit here," Sunny commanded, pulling out a chair. Gemma sat and Sunny rummaged in a cupboard. "I'm pretty sure Mom used...this!" She swung around holding a box of salt.

"Will that work?"

"It worked on Pepper. Why wouldn't it work on you? Hair's hair, right?"

Gemma shrugged. "I guess so."

Sunny stood behind Gemma and went to work massaging the salt into her hair. At first, she was gentle, trying to tease out pieces of hair gradually. When that didn't work, she began tugging. She yanked Gemma's head this way and that until Gemma felt as though her scalp might come off!

"Oww! What are you doing, Sunny?" she said, holding her head.

Sunny seemed to be speaking through gritted teeth. "Just a little more."

"I can't stand it! Is it almost out?"

Sunny came around and stood in front of Gemma examining her from the front. She put her hands on her hips.

"It's no use. I think, we're going to have to cut it out."

"What? You said your mum got it out of Pepper's hair!"

"I know. But maybe dog hair is different from human hair."

"Let's wait and see what your mum thinks."

"Do you want us to get in trouble?"

"No, but—"

The girls heard the back door bang open. Their eyes locked.

"It's Mom!" Sunny said, grabbing a tea towel. She threw it at Gemma. "Put that over your head. Quick!"

The tea towel hit Gemma in the face. She scrambled to position it on her head.

"Oh, it's only the boys," said Sunny, sounding relieved. "You can take that off, Gem."

Gemma took the tea towel from her hair as Dale and Landon appeared in the kitchen, along with two boys Gemma had never seen. They were wearing washed out T-shirts and cut-off jean shorts. The taller one had red hair and freckles, and the other one had biscuit-brown hair and freckles. They all stood gaping at Gemma. She willed the floor to open and swallow her whole, but nothing happened.

"Whoa," said Dale, eyeing Gemma's hair skeptically. "That didn't work."

"We're going to have to cut it out," Sunny said with authority.

The taller boy, the one with red hair, laughed. "No," he said. "You don't have to mutilate her. Use peanut butter. Remember when I got gum in Pepper's hair? Your mom used peanut butter to get it out."

"Oh, yeah!" Sunny said and rushed back to the cupboard.

"Gem, these are our cousins, Gordie and Brad," said Dale.

"Hey!" the boys said, with matching lop-sided grins. Gemma gave them a doleful smile and reached up to explore her hair. It felt like a shocking mess of grit and gum and twigs. She looked desperately at the boys and then at Sunny.

"Lucky we came in when we did, eh?" the taller one, Gordie, said, his voice ringing with laughter. "Or you might be bald."

"Yeah," Gemma said quietly. She was genuinely grateful to Gordie for saving her hair, but she still wished he and the other boys would go away.

Sunny returned with the peanut butter and began applying it to the top of Gemma's head as though she were icing a cake. The boys started laughing.

"You gotta use your hands, Sunny," Gordie said.

"I will!" Sunny said. "I know what I'm doing."

"It doesn't look like it," said Brad. The boys laughed.

"You guys can go now," Sunny told them.

"Come on, guys," Dale said, turning to leave the kitchen. The boys followed him out, talking and laughing about Gemma's close call.

It was a close call, Gemma thought. She tried to imagine her mother's reaction to a chunk of hair missing from the top of her head. A tear slid down her cheek, then another. Suddenly, she couldn't help herself; her shoulders were shaking, and she was sobbing.

"Why are you crying, Gem?" Sunny asked desperately. "The peanut butter is working. The gum is coming out. Really!"

Gemma wiped her eyes and started laughing and crying at the same time.

"I don't know why I'm crying," she said. "I guess I'm embarrassed. Or maybe I'm just relieved that we didn't have to cut my hair. I think...I think I miss my mum and dad!"

Sunny came around to face Gemma.

"Of course, you miss your parents," she said. "Come on. We'll go upstairs to finish getting the gum out. Then you can wash your hair."

Gemma nodded miserably and Sunny continued, "When Mom comes home, we'll ask her if you can call your parents. Would you like that?"

Gemma nodded and wiped her eyes again. She looked into Sunny's warm, friendly face and she couldn't help but smile. You suit your name, she thought.

Sunny smiled back and taking Gemma's hands in hers she pulled her out the chair.

"Okay, then," she said. "Let's go!"

CONGRATULATiONS!
YOU'VE READ **16,605** WORDS!

17

ater, in swimsuits and flip flops, with beach towels over their arms, Sunny and Gemma crossed the lawn and headed down to the lake. It was the middle of the day, and the sun was high in the sky.

Pepper lay on his side beneath a willow tree near the shore. He lifted his head as the girls drew near and thumped his tail a couple of times, but he didn't get up. Too hot! The boys were already in the water, shouting and playing.

"Is it warm?" Sunny called as she stepped onto the dock. Gemma followed, looking down into the water. The lake bottom was sandy and studded with stones. Tiny fish darted about in the shallows.

She wondered again what else might be lurking in the lake. Were there biting fish? She wanted to ask Sunny, but she was feeling a little shy again after her experience with the gum.

She had phoned her parents. No one answered. So, she left a message asking them to call. When she hung up, she felt lonely and glum.

Dale climbed onto the dock. "The water's great," he said. "Perfect for your first lake swim, Gem." He ran and dove off the end of the dock.

Gordie pulled himself up next. "Did you get the bubble gum out?" he asked Gemma.

She nodded and self-consciously ran her hand over her hair. The peanut butter had worked, but it had taken three attempts to wash out its oily residue, and even now she was sure she could smell it.

Gordie smiled and gave her two thumbs up, which made her feel a little better. Then he charged down the dock, and shouted, "Bombs away!" as he cannonballed into the water.

Gemma scanned the horizon.

"Is that an island?" she asked Sunny. She remembered seeing it earlier from her bed.

"Yeah, it's Summer Bug Island," Sunny said. "And this is Summer Bug Lake."

"Why is it called that?"

"Guess," Sunny said, swiping at a mosquito as it landed on her arm. Gemma smiled.

"Do you ever visit it?"

"All the time," said Sunny. "Some people say there's treasure buried on it. We've dug around for it, but we haven't found anything. One day soon we'll take you over there in the rowboat." She dove off the end of the dock.

Gemma wasn't ready to join her. She sat down and dipped her toes in the water to test it. It was warmer than she had expected it to be, and softer too. She still felt afraid, but she so loved water. Her curiosity was beginning to override her fear. She looked at the other kids having fun.

If I'm going to do any swimming this summer it's going to have to be in this lake, she thought. At that moment, Sunny popped her head out of the water.

"Come on, Gem! Jump in! It's really warm. Honest!"

Not wanting to let herself or her cousins down, Gemma smiled and got to her feet. She tossed her towel aside. Here I go, she thought. Taking a deep breath, she dove expertly into the water, hardly making a splash as she slipped beneath its surface.

The relief from the hot sun was instant and glorious and the deeper she dove, the cooler the water got. How different it is from diving into a swimming pool, she thought. She twisted and, kicking hard, swam back up.

"Well, what do you think?" Sunny asked as she broke through the surface. They treaded water together.

"It's brilliant," Gemma said. "It's so fresh and clean, and the water is so soft. I can't believe how the temperature changes as you go down."

"I know. Cold near the bottom, eh? And warm up here."

"Yes, I can feel the chill on my feet." Thinking of her feet put Gemma in mind of those biting fish again. "I saw some minnows by the dock. Are there big fish in here too?"

"No, just trout and bass."

"Do they bite?"

Sunny laughed and shook her head. "They're harmless."

Gemma smiled, took a deep breath, and ducked under the water again. She opened her eyes. It was murkier than the swimming baths. Instead of seeing bright blue light and other people's legs she saw the muted greens and browns of water, earth, and plants. It made her wonder if all her life she had been like a fish swimming in an aquarium. Out here, she felt wild and free, like a mermaid!

Bursting through the surface of the water she looked again for Sunny; she was standing on the dock.

"Wow! You sure can swim under water for a long time, Gem. I've never seen anyone hold their breath for that long."

Feeling invigorated, Gemma waved and ducked under again. She swam down and touched the silty bottom of the lake, then, kicking with all her might she followed the pale light filtering through the water back to the surface. Tonight, I shall need extra time to write in my journal, she thought. What a day!

That evening, Gemma hung up the phone in her aunt and uncle's study. Her parents had called her back, and she'd had a long chat with them. She felt better after hearing their voices. They laughed when she told them about the goats' playground and about her reunion with the dreaded chickens. She didn't tell them about the gum in her hair. It had worked out okay in the end, so she decided not to worry them with it.

While on the phone, she had been doodling in her journal. She closed it now and hugged it close to her chest. She was glad she had it to keep her company when she felt homesick or anxious.

I bet I'll need my journal tomorrow, she thought, as she made her way to bed. She was dreading tomorrow. Tomorrow, she would meet Bobbi.

CONGRATULATiONS!
YOU'VE READ **17,591** WORDS!

18

With packed lunches in hand, Sunny and Gemma headed outside to collect their bicycles. Gemma had her own bike. Uncle Roy got it for her, and he painted it purple. Her favourite colour!

Following Sunny along the shady drive of Almosta Farm, Gemma listened to the sound of gravel crunching beneath her bike tires. She wasn't used to riding on gravel. It was much more difficult than riding on pavement. She had to pay attention – especially on corners – to keep the bike steady and upright. Turning from the drive onto the gravel road, she gripped the handlebars tightly. Success, she thought, and pedalled on.

Be brave! Be brave! Be brave! Gemma reminded herself rhythmically, pumping her legs and pressing her feet hard against the pedals to keep up with Sunny. They were on their way to Bobbi's house and Gemma felt nervous. All sorts of possibilities had tormented her since hearing that Sunny's cousin, Bobbi, was also her best friend. Most of all: What if she doesn't like me?

Catching up to Sunny, she asked, "What are we going to do today?"

"We'll see what Bobbi wants to do. She's always got good ideas."

Gemma pedalled harder, her nervous energy propelling her bicycle quickly up a steep hill.

"Hey! Wait up!" Sunny called. "We're almost there."

They crested the hill and Gemma saw Bobbi's green house in the distance. As they drew closer, a figure jumped up from the porch, got on a bike, and began cycling fast down a long driveway.

"Hey Bobbi!" Sunny called when they were almost upon the driveway.

Gemma looked at the girl lounging on a red bike at the end of the drive. She was tall and lanky, dressed in a red T-shirt and blue shorts. Her strawberry blond hair was pulled into a stubby ponytail at the base of her skull. She kicked up her foot, showing off a white and blue running shoe. Looking at Sunny, she called out, "Got them yesterday and they're still clean. Mom is amazed. What do you think?"

"Cool!" said Sunny, skidding to a stop. "How was your day at the mall?"

The girl shrugged and dropped a paper lunch bag into Sunny's basket; her bike didn't have a basket.

"Boring, mostly," she said. "Ashley dragged us into lots of clothing stores."

So, Bobbi thought buying clothes was boring. Uh-oh, thought Gemma. That's the first thing we don't have in common. When she came to a stop, Sunny turned and smiled at her.

"Gemma, this is my cousin, Bobbi. Bobbi, this is my cousin, Gemma," she said, indicating each of them playfully.

"Hello," said Gemma, with a shy smile. Seeing Bobbi's blue eyes appraising her, she tightened her grip on her handlebars.

"Hi," Bobbi said, flashing her a cool smile. "Let's get going. We can talk while we ride."

Bobbi took the lead. Once she had picked up speed she let go of the handlebars and sat up straight, resting her hands on her thighs.

"Having a good time?" she asked.

"Yes, I like it here," Gemma said. She tried to mimic Bobbi's cool demeanor, but she suspected she was too preoccupied with keeping her bike steady to pull it off.

How is she able to ride with no hands when she's on gravel? Gemma wondered. I can't even do it on pavement.

"Been swimming yet?" asked Bobbi.

"Gem is an amazing swimmer!" Sunny said. "You should see how long she can hold her breath under water."

"Oh, yeah?" Bobbi looked down her nose at Gemma, as though she might be considering some sort of contest.

"Gem, tell Bobbi what happened to you on the airplane when you were coming over. You'll love this, Bobbi!"

Gemma retold the story of Baby Henry. Bobbi laughed. Feeling encouraged, she went on to tell her about Landon knocking over his water at the dinner table and drenching her new pajamas. She was beginning to feel like quite a comedian, playing up all the comical aspects. By the end, Bobbi was laughing so hard she had to grab the handlebars of her bike.

"Guess you're going to *soak up* as much of Canada as you can, eh?" Bobbi snorted. Sunny groaned. Gemma laughed. She liked a good pun.

They rode on three abreast. Gemma felt more and more at ease. She sensed that her adventures, and the way she had handled herself in tricky situations, impressed Bobbi. Each time Bobbi spoke, she now made eye contact with Gemma as well as Sunny.

"Where do you guys want to go?" Sunny asked. "That sun is getting really hot."

"Let's go check out the abandoned house," said Bobbi. "We haven't been there in a while."

"Good idea!" said Sunny. She looked at Gemma. "Technically, it's off limits but everybody goes there."

"Is it far?" asked Gemma. She was thirsty, and she was beginning to feel hungry too.

"Just around the next corner," Bobbi said.

They had to pedal up another hill before they turned the corner and Gemma saw what she guessed was their destination: A dilapidated two-story wooden house, standing in a meadow before a tall, leafy tree.

CONGRATULATIONS!
YOU'VE READ **18,447** WORDS!

19

Gemma followed the girls along a well-trodden, bumpy path through knee-high grass and wildflowers. The air around them was heavy and sweetly scented, thrumming with the sound of insects at work. Without the breeze their cycling had created, the sun was suddenly unbearably hot. Gemma longed for shade and a cool drink.

"We'll hide our bikes around back," Bobbi said over her shoulder. The girls followed her, dropping their bikes in the tall grass beneath the tree.

"Ah, that shade feels good," Gemma said, wiping her brow. "Is anyone else dreadfully thirsty?"

"Dreadfully!" Bobbi said, smiling cheerfully as she imitated Gemma's accent.

"Do I really sound like that?" Gemma asked, after taking a long drink from her water bottle.

"Not really," Sunny said with a laugh. "Well, sort of, but I like your accent!"

"Me too," said Bobbi. "I wish I had an accent."

Gemma gave Bobbi a questioning look. "You have an accent. You have a Canadian accent."

"Canadians don't have accents."

"Of course, they do! If you went to England people would know you were from Canada by the way you talk. That's all an accent is; same words, different sounds."

Bobbi shrugged. "I guess you're right. I never really thought about it like that."

Gemma smiled. "Shall we have our lunch now?" she asked hopefully.

"Let's look around first and then we'll eat," Sunny said, putting away her water bottle.

The girls picked their way through the tall grass and Bobbi shoved open a back door. They stepped into a modest kitchen. Its furnishings were long gone. The cupboard doors were either missing or standing open, and the floor was covered in dirty, curling linoleum.

"We haven't come here in ages," Sunny said softly. "I'd forgotten how spooky it is."

Bobbi said, "What's spooky about it?"

"Somebody else could be here already," Sunny murmured. "They could be spying on us right now." She and Gemma exchanged uneasy glances.

Bobbi rolled her eyes and the girls continued cautiously into the living room. A fireplace mantle and peeling floral wallpaper were the only evidence that anyone had once lived there. The girls continued their exploration, climbing a rickety staircase. Upstairs, they found three empty bedrooms and a filthy bathroom.

"Worse than I remembered," Bobbi said with a sigh. "Let's go eat."

She started back downstairs. Sunny and Gemma took a last look around. They ran from bedroom to bedroom, trying to imagine who might have lived there. They talked about how they would decorate. They were leaning out two windows, waving to each other, when they heard a terrible crack!

"Bobbi?" Sunny shouted, running to the top of the stairs. Gemma was hot on her heels. "Bobbi? Are you okay?"

"I'm stuck!" Bobbi called. The girls flew down the stairs and into the kitchen.

"What happened?" they cried in unison. Bobbi sat with her foot through a hole in the kitchen floor.

"The floor felt spongy here, like a trampoline, so I just started jumping on it and my foot went right through. I got my leg out, but I can't get my foot out." She looked around. "We'd better get out of here before the whole place collapses," she said dramatically.

Sunny and Gemma cast anxious glances around the kitchen. They crept cautiously towards Bobbi. Sunny bent down, taking her under the arm.

"Gemma, you take Bobbi's other arm, and we'll pull. Ready?" Gemma nodded and did as Sunny said. They yanked while Bobbi wriggled her foot. When it came free they all toppled over backwards.

"Nooo," wailed Bobbi, closing her eyes, and throwing her head back.

"Are you hurt?" Sunny asked.

"No! Look!" Bobbi pointed. Her new running shoe was missing. "Mom's gonna be so mad at me! We've got to get my shoe back."

"How?" said Sunny. "We don't even know where it is."

"It must be in the basement. We'll have to go down there."

Sunny's eyes bugged out. "I'm not going down there!"

"What's a basement?" Gemma asked. For a moment, the girls seemed to forget their predicament. They looked at Gemma.

"What do you mean?" Bobbi said. "What do you call the rooms under your house if they're not a basement?"

Gemma shrugged. "We don't have rooms under our house. Neither does anyone I know."

"Weird," said Bobbi. "Here, most people have rooms under their houses."

"Weird," Gemma echoed.

"Now that you mention it, it does sound a bit weird," Bobbi said. She laughed.

"What are you two talking about?" Sunny demanded, slapping her hands against her thighs. "We can't go down into that basement, Bobbi. There are rats down there!"

Sunny and Bobbi had once crept down the outside steps of the abandoned house and poked their heads into the root cellar below. It smelled damp and dirty. Through the dim light they could see that the walls were made of boulders and rubble. Sunny had heard nothing, but Bobbi convinced her that she had heard rats rustling about and squeaking.

"Rats?" Gemma shuddered.

"Bobbi said she saw rats the last time we went down there," Sunny said.

"I said I thought I might have *heard* rats," Bobbi said. "Anyway, it wouldn't matter if there were alligators down there. I've got to go and get my shoe back and you've got to come with me."

"No way!" Sunny said.

"You have to!" Bobbi pleaded. "How am I supposed to ride my bike without a shoe? If I go home without that shoe, I'll be grounded for a week."

Sunny's face crumpled. "I can't go down there, Bobbi. It's too creepy!"

Bobbi glowered for a moment. "Okay, be a baby. I'll go by myself." She got up and marched, as best she could with only one shoe, back outside. Sunny and Gemma ran after her.

"Wait," said Sunny. Bobbi stopped.

"Gemma and I will go with you, but we won't go in. We'll stand on the steps outside." Gemma nodded enthusiastically. She had no wish to go into another small dark space, especially one with rats.

Bobbi glared at them for a moment. "Fine!" she said and marched on. When she reached the steps, she hesitated for a moment, and then she charged down and disappeared through a low doorway.

Sunny and Gemma crept down the stairs holding onto each other. They stood in the doorway, listening to Bobbi rustling around in the root cellar. Sunny leaned in for a closer look and they heard a muffled, "Oomph!"

CONGRATULATIONS!
YOU'VE READ **19,522** WORDS!

20

"Bobbi?" Sunny cried, digging her fingernails deep into Gemma's forearm. "Where are you?"

When there was no reply, Gemma whispered, "What shall we do?"

"We have to go in," Sunny said, digging her nails deeper into Gemma's arm. "We have to go get her."

Trembling, they looked at each other with bulging eyes.

"Bobbi?" Sunny squeaked again, as she and Gemma stepped over the threshold into the blackness. They heard rustling. Was it rats? Or something worse?

"Bobbi," both girls whispered desperately. They took another step and a hand shot out.

"Ahhh!" Screaming, they turned and fled back up the stairs. Raucous laughter chased them.

"You two are hilarious," Bobbi said, emerging into the sunlight. She held up her shoe. "Got it! And it's still clean!"

"Bobbi!" Sunny stamped her foot. "How could you? I almost had a heart attack!"

"Serves you right," said Bobbi, scowling and squinting in the sunlight. "You should've come with me. There could've been anything down there."

Gemma, her heart pounding, and her legs wobbling like jelly, slumped onto the grass. She examined her arm where Sunny had clawed her.

"That was so mean, Bobbi, and not funny at all," scolded Sunny. She put her hands on her hips in a move reminiscent of Aunt Linda. "Look what you've done! You've terrified Gemma! And she's bleeding!"

"How'd that happen?" Bobbi asked, pulling on her shoe.

"I scratched her when you scared us."

"Then you did it, not me."

"It wouldn't have happened if you hadn't been so mean."

"I'm okay," Gemma said. Truthfully, she felt badly shaken, but the last thing she wanted was for Sunny and Bobbi to start fighting on account of her.

"Let's have lunch and forget about it," she said, forcing a smile and getting to her feet. "I'm okay. Really. It's just a scratch."

Sunny and Bobbi glared at each other, then without another word the girls returned to their bikes, retrieved their packed lunches, and sat down under the tree. Unwrapping their sandwiches, they ate in sullen silence. Gemma kept her eyes on her food because she didn't know where to look.

She had almost finished her sandwich when Bobbi surprised her by muttering, "Sorry I scared you, Gem. Is your arm okay?"

She looked up. Bobbi smiled shyly at her.

You really are courageous, Gemma thought. Not only did you go into that basement by yourself, but you can even say you're sorry when you're wrong.

"It's okay. I'm fine," she said. "Thank you, Bobbi."

"What about me?" demanded Sunny.

Bobbi shrugged and chewed another couple of bites of her sandwich. Then she barked at Sunny, "Okay, I'm sorry I scared you, Sunny. But I still think you should have come with me. What if there was something terrible down there?"

"Yeah, well, sorry I let you go in. I should've stopped you."

"As if you could," Bobbi said, punching Sunny's shoulder playfully and laughing. Sunny laughed too.

Much to Gemma's relief, the girls seemed willing to leave it at that. The atmosphere lightened and they went on with their picnic.

"I'm still hungry," Sunny said when she had finished her sandwich and apple. She nibbled all around the apple's tiny seed casing and threw what was left of it into the tall grass. "I wish we had some of your brookies, Bobbi."

Bobbi raised her brows and reached into her lunch bag.

"Lucky for you, you're being nice to me," she said, bringing out a little parcel wrapped in wax paper. Sunny clapped excitedly.

"You did bring them!"

Bobbi opened the parcel to reveal three big cookies. They were covered in a layer of chocolate.

"Sorry they're a bit squished and melted," she said, offering them around.

"I don't care," Sunny said, taking one. "Thanks!"

'Thank you," said Gemma.

Biting into the cookie, Gemma's taste buds went wild. "This is gorgeous!" she said. "It's the fudgiest, most delicious cookie I've ever had. Why do you call them brookies?"

Bobbi grinned. "Because they're brownies and cookies combined. It's my own secret recipe."

"I know the recipe," Sunny quipped.

"Yeah, but you're sworn to secrecy."

Sunny shrugged and nodded. Gemma suddenly felt like an outsider again. She concentrated on eating her brookie.

"Bobbi's going to open a bakery someday," Sunny said.

"Are you?" said Gemma.

Bobbi nodded. "It's going to be all chocolate stuff, because that's what I like best."

"Me too," said Gemma, popping her final bite of brookie into her mouth. "You'll sell lots of these. They're fab! I bet you'll become famous."

Bobbi smiled and gave Gemma another of her appraising looks.

"Can you keep a secret?" she asked.

Sunny interjected, "Gem is totally trustworthy. We pinky promised not to look in each other's diaries, and I know she hasn't touched mine." She looked at Gemma. "Don't worry, I haven't touched yours either."

"I know." Gemma smiled.

"You like baking, Gem?" Bobbi asked.

"I love it!"

"Come to my place one day and we'll make brookies together."

"Thanks!" said Gemma eagerly.

Feeling emboldened by Bobbi's offer, Gemma made one of her own. "If you want, I can show you how to make Banoffee Pie."

"Banoffee Pie?" Sunny and Bobbi chorused.

"Bananas and cream and brown sugar and chocolate all made into a scrumptious biscuity pie. My friend Bronwyn and I used to make it together."

"Count me in," said Bobbi, getting up and brushing grass off the seat of her pants.

"Sounds amazing," said Sunny, doing the same.

As the girls gathered their lunch things and put them back into their bike baskets, Bobbi asked Gemma about Bronwyn. She was sympathetic when Gemma told her about Bronwyn moving to Australia. She understood, too, when she said she had no wish to go to day camp on her own.

"It's so lonely and scary without your best friend," Gemma said.

"Yes," Bobbi said with feeling. She looked at Gemma for another moment, and then blurted, "I was really worried when I heard you were coming. I didn't know if you'd like me, or if I'd like you. And with Sunny being my best friend..." Her words trailed off and she shrugged.

Gemma laughed nervously. "That's exactly how I felt. I was worried we might not get along, but—"

"We do!" Bobbi said, swinging her leg over her bike. "I think you're cool."

"I think you're cool, too," Gemma said, pulling her bike up from the grass.

"I knew you'd like each other," Sunny said, getting onto her bike. "Why wouldn't you? You're both super cool and you're cousins." She started pedalling back toward the path. "Come on," she called over her shoulder. "I want to go swimming."

Bobbi and Gemma looked at each other.

"We're not actually cousins," Bobbi said, turning her gaze to Sunny's retreating back. "My dad is Sunny's mom's brother. Your dad is her dad's brother. So, we're not related. There's no blood between us."

Gemma nodded, feeling a touch of awkwardness creeping up her spine. But something in Bobbi's profile prompted her to squash it.

"There's no blood," Gemma said. "But that doesn't mean we can't still be family...if we want to be."

Bobbi looked at her again. She grinned. "Okay, cuz!" she said, pushing down on her bike pedal and starting off after Sunny.

Riding back to Almosta Farm was easy. The girls coasted down the big hills that had been so much work to climb on their way to the abandoned house. They smiled at one another, shouting encouragement as they sailed home.

As she reached the bottom of the hill, Gemma pedalled hard to keep up the momentum. She felt giddy with excitement and relief. She was becoming more and more confident riding her bicycle on gravel, and she and Bobbi were friends.

Her thoughts turned to the other challenges she had faced since saying goodbye to her parents. So much had happened already – both good and bad – and so much more would happen. She had the whole summer ahead of her. But I can handle it, she thought. I'm capable! Biting her lip, she steadied herself, and looking straight ahead, she took her hands off the handlebars – for a moment!

CONGRATULATIONS!

YOU'VE READ A GRAND TOTAL OF 20,884 WORDS!

This QR code will take
you to our website:

WWW.HEATHERNQUINN.COM

You're the engine that powers
My Country Cousins!

Books are like people. Some we love. Some we like. Some we're not keen on.

If you liked *Journey to Juniper Junction*, please take a moment now to visit your on-line retailer and leave a review. Reader reviews are the lifeblood of books in the 21st century.

If you didn't like *Journey to Juniper Junction*, would you be so kind as to send us an email and let us know why? Tell us what you thought was missing. We're just like you! We are always learning, and we appreciate constructive criticism. Under 13? Please, ask your parent or guardian for permission to contact us.

We've written a short story just for you!

Learn more about Gemma's life in England and her best friend, Bronwyn, in *Goodbye, Bronwyn*, the short story prequel to *Journey to Juniper Junction*.

To get *Goodbye, Bronwyn* follow these steps:

1. Visit our website www.heathernquinn.com
2. Input your email address (We won't share it.)
3. Hit send and watch your inbox. If your copy of *Goodbye, Bronwyn* doesn't appear, please check your spam folder, and whitelist our IP address. Thanks!

We'd love to hear from you!

We enjoy getting letters and drawings from our readers, so we've set up a special post box just for you:

Heather N. Quinn
c/o Babblegarden Publishing Ltd.
P.O. Box 58, Navan Stn Main
Navan, Ontario, Canada
K4B 1J3

Or you can email us at hello@heathernquinn.com

If you're under 13, please talk to your mum or dad, or whoever looks after you, before you input your e-mail.

Thanks, kids!

ABOUT HEATHER N. QUINN

Heather N. Quinn is the pen name of the mother and daughter writing team Heather and Quinn. **My Country Cousins** grew out of their shared love of lighthearted fiction and family life.

Please visit their website at www.heathernquinn.com to learn more about Heather and Quinn and the **My Country Cousins** series.

ACKNOWLEDGEMENTS

It's remarkable how much work goes into producing even a small book like *Journey to Juniper Junction*. Fortunately, we enjoyed doing it, and we got a lot of help along the way.

Our families have been so loving and supportive. Thanks, everyone! You make life so much fun!

A big shout out to our mentor, April Cox! April helped us to understand and navigate the publishing world with grace and aplomb. She also introduced us to Kit Laurence Nacua, our talented cover illustrator, and Praise Saflor, our clever book designer. Working with all of you has been such a treat.

Special thanks to our editors and to everyone who read our book and offered their feedback. What a difference your contributions made!

Readers, you deserve a great big thank you too! Your imagination is what brings Gemma Merriman and her family and friends to life. So, thank you for reading! We hope you enjoyed the story.

STAY TUNED!
COMING SOON!

My Country Cousins

BOOK 2

ADVENTURES AT ALMOSTA FARM

Visit us at www.heathernquinn.com to find out what Gemma and the Merriman gang get up to in our second book, *Adventures at Almosta Farm*. While you're there, sign up for *Goodbye, Bronwyn*, a short story prequel to *Journey to Juniper Junction*. You'll learn about Gemma's life in England and find out why she and her lifelong bestie, Bronwyn, must say goodbye.

(Under 13? Please, ask your parent or guardian for permission to request the story. Thanks, kids!)

Made in the USA
Columbia, SC
15 July 2021